Secrets of Capell Manor

by

Beth Ann Price

Secrets of Capell Manor

COPYRIGHT © 2025 by Beth Ann Price

Cover Art by *Teddi Black*

The Wild Rose Press, Inc.
PO Box 708
Adams Basin, NY 14410-0708
Visit us at www.thewildrosepress.com

Publishing History
First Edition, 2025
Trade Paperback ISBN 978-1-5092-6304-2
Digital ISBN 978-1-5092-6305-9

Published in the United States of America

Dedication

To my husband and family for your unwavering support
and encouragement.
I couldn't have done this without you.
And especially to my mom, who taught me to always
try new things and to live a life free of regrets.

Prologue

Lord Edmond Capell squinted at the blurred markings on the cards; his meaty hand trembled as he held them. He'd lost again. With a grunt of frustration, the old lord flung the cards across the table, scattering them like leaves in the wind. Nervous beads of sweat glistened on his brow; his stomach twisted in a sickly churn.

"Pay up, Capell!" his associate slurred, the words tumbling out in a half-belch.

Capell looked down and realized that all his coins would be cleaned out with this loss. He sighed and reached for his mug of ale. But rather than retrieving it, he pushed it over clumsily, and the dark liquid spilled across the table and dripped to the floor.

"And don't forget what you already owe me," the younger man bellowed. "I want every last bit of it tonight!"

Sweat now dripped down his back and pooled under his arms. Through his alcohol-induced haze, he knew the man who sat across from him was dead serious. He feared he might not live much longer if he didn't pay.

"Come on, man! You know I'll make good on what I owe. I just need a little more time."

His plea was met with a piercing glance and cold smirk as much as his drunken friend could muster.

Capell shook his head. "One more hand?"

"Why should I play another hand, old man? I've already won!"

Capell's alcohol-soaked brain scrambled for a solution—something that would give him one last chance. He tried to sit up a bit taller, but he only swayed over in his chair. He grabbed the edge of the table and finally managed to say, "I'll make the deal sweeter. If I lose, I'll give you what you've been hounding me for the last months."

The young man's interest piqued, and he sat up straight. "And if I lose?"

"Then my debt to you is erased, and I'll hear no more of it."

There was only a brief pause, but then the young man looked Edmond dead in the eyes and said, "Deal the cards, old man."

Chapter One

England, 1638

The slap from his open hand against her face rang out through her upper chamber. The raised imprint on her left cheek burned and pain radiated through her skull as her head snapped back. The floor rose up to meet her as she fell with a solid *thump*. She opened her eyes and looked up at her uncle. Saliva spewed from his mouth as he yelled curses down upon her, but her ears rang so loud that she could barely make out his foul tirade.

"You filthy beggar wench! You've always been ungrateful!" he screamed with slurred words as she crawled away from him on the floor.

"Uncle! Stop!" Lady Rosalind screamed. She'd crawled as far as she could and was now pressed against the wall. She shielded her face and made herself as small as possible.

With drunken utterances, the lord of the manor continued his rant and she gagged with the smell of his rancid breath as his rage spewed from his mouth,

"I've fed you. Clothed you. And given you a roof over your head. You miserable lout! You should be grateful for whatever I give you and do what I say!"

Rosalind, usually hesitant to argue in retaliation against her guardian, could not hold her tongue this time. "Yes, you have, Uncle. But not willingly! The king made you take me in. And it's not as if I came with nothing! You had my father's money and squandered all of it! Now I have nothing!

Lord Edmond's face turned even redder, and a vein bulged and pulsed on his forehead. She pressed harder against the wall and braced herself for another blow.

"I won't do it! I won't! And the king would never approve! I would rather die!" Her last words were spoken through clenched teeth.

Edmond responded with a roar and threw her back onto the floor. "You may get your wish, harlot!" As his boot came down to stomp her face, in his drunken state, he lost his balance, stumbled, and fell. Rosalind saw her chance and crawled rapidly from her chamber.

She pulled herself to her feet and ran. Down the stairs, she flew. She both hoped and feared that he would follow her. He was out of control, and he might turn his aggression on the children. She grabbed her cloak that hung by the door leading outside from the kitchen and ran toward the stable as fast as she could.

She bridled her mare but didn't bother with a saddle. She climbed upon Mercy's slick back and urged her into a gallop, going as fast as she could safely traverse the dirt road leading away from the manor on the moonless night.

It seemed only a few minutes passed and bile rose in her throat, and her heart jumped as the sound of pounding hooves rose up behind her.

****

Capell Manor, Three Weeks Later

The cold wind bit at Devlin Alastor's face, cutting through his cloak as he sat atop his horse, looking down at the manor below. The night was heavy with mist, the chill creeping into his bones despite the layers he wore. His breath formed clouds in the air, dissolving into the fog as quickly as they appeared. He had been sent to Capell Manor on yet another mission for King Charles I, while a memory of blue terror-stricken eyes still haunted him.

Two weeks ago, he'd ridden through a similar mist to a small village to find Thomas Davies, a man accused of treason. Devlin closed his eyes, and the scene returned to him in vivid detail—the small cottage with a hole in the roof, the desperate pleading, and the sharp, final sound of his blade meeting flesh.

He could still see Thomas's eyes, wide with fear and resignation, as he raised his sword. The man's last words echoed in his ears, a futile plea for mercy that Devlin had ignored without a second thought. After all, it wasn't his place to judge this man guilty or innocent. The king and his council had done so. That mission was like so many others. The man was ruled guilty; he had fled and was in hiding. Devlin's job was to find him, kill him, and return to the king with his head. It was another life taken and another duty fulfilled.

But this time, it didn't feel routine.

Devlin shifted in his saddle; the images ran through his mind over and over. Davies had begged for his life. That wasn't unusual—most men did when they faced their death. But after his sword had severed the man's head from his body, he had stepped back, his task complete, only to find himself facing a sight now burned into his memory—a child standing in the doorway, her blue eyes wide and unblinking. Her tiny hands clutched a worn doll, and she couldn't have been more than five years old. The terror in her eyes was unlike anything Devlin had ever seen.

Time stopped in that moment; her gaze moved from her father's head, which had rolled close to her feet to Devlin's eyes, piercing through him, seeing not a knight in service to the king but a monster who had taken her father away. For the first time, he had seen himself through the eyes of an innocent, and it was a vision he could not shake.

Devlin exhaled sharply, the cold air stinging his lungs. The king's orders had been clear; the evidence of Thomas's guilt was unconvincing, but the command was absolute. Disobedience was not an option. Yet, as he sat on that hill overlooking Capell Manor waiting for his next mission to begin, the weight of that moment pressed down upon him.

He had not spoken of it, not even to Alden. There was no point. It would change nothing. The king would continue to command, and he would continue to obey, but the child's eyes haunted him, lingering in the shadows of his thoughts. They made him question, even if just for a fleeting moment, the endless cycle of violence he had been bound to for so long. What kind of man had he become to carry out such orders without question? And what kind of man would he be if he did not?

But nothing could be done now. While the king valued his loyalty and seemed to appreciate that he got him out of many scandals and scrapes, a man of his lowly station had few choices. He was bound to a life of completing unsavory tasks. The son of a hired mercenary, it was only natural that he continued in his father's footsteps.

He was a killer for hire, and the pay was good. After all, what else could he have done? Been a farmer? A sarcastic "huh" escaped his lips.

Many pointed to his surname's meaning: avenger. And that alone somehow destined him to a life of avenging his king's honor. No one would argue he was both brave and even menacing. He had never lost a battle and had never been bested in a fight. His reputation had made him a popular man whom many sought to retain his services or for revenge, but he served only one man, and no one questioned his loyalty.

But ironically, his given name could be translated as 'unlucky,' too, and he was beginning to think that his luck was running out as he sat high atop a hill on a cold January night with the ghostly visage of blue eyes and the sound of a head falling to the floor haunting him.

Occasionally, the thick clouds parted, allowing the full moon to briefly shine through before being obscured again by the dark, shifting sky. Yet, the misty cold rain persisted, soaking through his boots and creeping upward with a chill that slowly sank into his bones. He cursed silently under his breath.

He often contemplated abandoning this wretched existence, but the king always dangled the prospect of reward before him—his own lands and a home in exchange for his unwavering loyalty and his readiness to undertake the most unpleasant tasks without question or hesitation.

Now, he wondered if this mission might prove the most distasteful of all.

So a day when he wasn't running hither and yon chasing down the king's enemies seemed far out of his reach. And who knew if the king would fulfill the promise of land and home? Devlin pondered this thought as he grew cold sitting on his steed.

What in the name of all that's holy am I doing here?

"Cursed rain!" Alden sighed loudly in frustration and anger. "What in the bloody hell are we doing here?" Alden, his best and only friend, and also his second-in-command, echoed his own thoughts.

"We are, my dear fellow, here to find the elusive Sir Edmond, as it seems our king has once again misplaced one of his loyal subjects. We are to discover the reason for his absence," Devlin replied, not without sarcasm. "This earl, Edmond Capell, did not arrive at court after a summons was delivered to him. The king waited seven days and is now wondering where he is. Our job is to find him and deliver him to the king post-haste, whether he wants to come or not."

Ignoring a summons from the king was a serious offense. Lesser insubordinations and insults often resulted in being jailed or even hanged. But the king did not suspect Lord Edmond had struck out on his own to conspire against him. He suspected foul play, not a disobedient lord. Edmond had always been a staunch supporter. Although he had a questionable character, he had never given reason to doubt his steadfast devotion to the king and country.

"So what do we know?" Alden asked.

"We know that the king commanded Capell to appear in court some twenty-one days ago. He was expected in the first week of January, but he failed to arrive when expected. He had replied with a message of his own that he was honored to be invited to court and would be there. The king waited, as you know, but Lord

Edmond Capell never made it to the palace. And that is all we know about Lord Edmond," said Devlin.

"And what about the manor house? What are we walking into there?" Devin looked down at the manor house. He saw no fires in the courtyard. Further, there were no men in the watchtower. That alone didn't bode well. King Charles had warned his Royalists to remain vigilant. No loyal servant to the king would leave his house and land without even a minimal guard.

He looked down at his loyal hound, Grim, who stood to the side of his steed. The large dog detected no movement outside the manor house.

"Lord Edmond Capell, from what I gather, is a lecherous old man who loves games of chance. He is rumored to be loose with his money at the gaming tables and likewise likes loose women. I have heard he has quite the temper and runs his house on the bare minimum needed to keep the manor afloat. His servants hate him, and he has no family except a niece over whom he has guardianship."

"He once kept a small regiment of men here with him, but he failed to pay them so many times that they left. He relies on the king for protection now."

Both men were silent for a moment. "This lord doesn't sound like much of anything. Why does the king have so much interest in finding him?" Alden wondered out loud.

"His lands lay next to those of several men whose loyalty the king considers questionable. Suffice it to say, Lord Edmond keeps a close watch and reports anything suspicious directly to His Majesty." Sir Devlin paused, weighing his words with care. "But it's not my place to challenge the king's urgency in this matter. I have my orders, and I intend to carry them out."

Alden thought for a moment and then asked, "What of the niece?"

"What of her?" Devlin responded. "Her lot in life, most assuredly, has not been easy. But that's not my problem. Hopefully, she'll have some information we can use to clear up this mess. And if not, she'll discover quickly; it's best not to hinder my investigation. I want to resolve this as quickly as possible."

A sharp wind blew. Alden shivered as the cold draft forced its way through his heavily padded doublet and cape. Devlin refused to tremble, refused to show weakness. He countenance was emotionless, like stone; his eyes faced forward to the manor house below.

Devlin picked up his horse's reins. His mount, after standing in the wind, raised his head and let out an impatient snort.

And without a word, Devlin began a careful descent down the hill toward the manor house.

****

Rosalind sat in a comfortable rocking chair in front of the large fire in the great room. The hearth was massive—a fully-grown adult could walk easily inside the firebox without striking the stones above, and its flames provided generous warmth for the dining hall. However, the roaring blaze did nothing to warm her this evening. Fear had settled deeply into her bones.

Marta, the cook, sat with her and watched the flames dance in the hearth. Her normally cheerful round face was drawn with worry. Marta was more of a mother to Rosalind than anyone else in her life. Rosalind knew Marta loved her like her own and had refused to leave her alone to face the beast.

An hour had passed since Ridley had run roughshod out the kitchen door and around the corner, bringing the news she had so dreaded. He yelled loudly, "They're here!"

The loyal kitchen boy had kept careful watch for two days, knowing the king's men would arrive.

And despite the knowledge of their upcoming arrival, her breath hitched, and her stomach threatened to empty itself of the little amount of food she had managed to eat that day. She stood at Ridley's announcement but the room spun slightly and a cold sweat popped out on her brow.

"My lady! Sit before you faint!"

Rosalind took a deep breath. "I am fine," she said in a weak voice. But she sat with shaky knees. "Ridley, tell me how many and what they are doing."

"Milady, there are two men at the top of Knobs Hill looking down upon the manor. One is tall with light hair. The other is as dark as midnight. Black hair and he looks fierce. He is dressed all in black, and his horse is black as well."

Cold dread and then a feeling of doom hit her. Marta held her hand to her mouth to stifle a gasp.

"And beside his steed, a large hound sits looking mean as the devil. He could eat me in one bite for sure!"

"Ridley," Rosalind said firmly, "Let's not let our imagination interfere with our assessment. The simple facts are hard enough to deal with right now."

But Rosalind knew who this rider was. His reputation preceded him. Sir Devlin Alastor. A loyal servant and hired killer of the king. Rumors abound wherever he went. It was said he killed without mercy and enjoyed what he did. Her worst nightmare had come true. She had prayed fervently for the king to send a harmless clerk or even a local sheriff to look for Lord Edmond, but instead, she would now face the devil himself.

"They are just sitting there milady. Just watching."

And so she waited. The few house servants she had left had prepared the manor house for visitors. The guest rooms were aired. Wood for fires was stacked in the rooms, and a bathtub was ready for use should the king's men wish to bathe. But more important than readying the manor was that they all had to be mentally prepared. They had to appear unafraid and as perplexed as anyone over Lord Edmond's disappearance.

Everyone had to tell the king's men the same story. The slightest inconsistency could spell doom for them all.

Her heart beat quickened when her uncle's manservant entered the hall. Benton had served the Capell family for three generations. No one knew how old he was, but Ridley often joked he was at least one-hundred-and-twenty.

He walked painfully slow across the great room. His once tall, proud stature was now bent over in the shoulders. And Benton never hurried. In fact, he was probably unable to hurry at his great age. But Rosalind considered him a great treasure. His wisdom and quick wit had got her out of many unfortunate circumstances.

"My lady," he said calmly, "The king's men have arrived."

Rosalind swallowed hard. A bead of cold sweat traveled down her back, and once again, a wave of nausea shot through her abdomen.

Pull yourself together! Losing your dinner at the feet of the king's men is not the first impression you wish to make. Breathe! Breathe!

After a moment, she said in a steady voice, "Show them in, Benton."

Benton gave a curt nod, turned, and walked just as slowly out of the room as he had walked in.

Did anything rattle that man?

Rosalind looked down and she was wringing her hands to keep them from shaking.

Oh, Lord, Father in Heaven. Hear my prayer. Deliver me from this evil and keep my family safe from harm...

As she prayed, her breathing calmed slightly. From across the grand hall, the heavy English double doors creaked open with a slow, ominous wail that echoed through the lower rooms of the manor. Silence followed, thick and suffocating, until the doors groaned shut once more. A cold draft curled around her feet, but the chill that crept up her spine came from something far more unsettling than the icy air.

Two men rounded the corner from the manor's foyer and entered the great room. Just as Ridley described, one man stood almost a head taller than his companion and his skin and eyes were fair. He looked cold, but his face was not unpleasant, just tinged red with the damp chill of the evening. His eyes were a clear blue, and his beard, trimmed in the Norman fashion, framed his jaw. His hair under his helmet appeared to be a light brown, almost the color of honey, and wet.

His companion stood in stark, foreboding contrast to his tall, fair friend.

He was not overly tall, but his dark presence commanded attention, and Rosalind's breathing threatened to get out of control again quickly. He was a wall of black from head to toe. He wore black clothing, boots, and a cloak. The clothes did not conceal the raw strength shown in his muscled arms and broad chest. On his face, a scar ran from the corner of his right eye, passed down his cheek, and ended at the corner of his mouth—a full mouth that wore a frown when he entered the room.

A shadow, an evil shadow. Now, whose imagination is running amok?

Benton's strong voice broke into her thoughts.

"Lady Rosalind Capell, I present Sir Devlin Alastor and Alden Danby."

She wasn't sure how she managed, but she stood from her chair without the slightest wobble.

"Sir Devlin, Mr. Danby," she said with a slight nod. "Please come in and warm yourself by the fire."

As the men moved toward the hearth, she turned to Marta, "Marta, please fetch some warmed cider or ale for our guests."

Poor Marta nearly went down on her first step. Their brave act threatened to dissolve already. Ridley was there to offer his help.

"Now Mum, I see your lame knee is botherin' ya. Let me help you to the kitchen."

Clever Ridley…

The men removed their cloaks, and Benton took them to hang where they could dry. They walked to the edge of the hearth and stretched their hands toward the flames, but the dark one did not stay there long. He paced around the room.

Rosalind's gaze turned to the ominous figure as he assessed his surroundings.

"Sir Devlin," she said tentatively. "Please sit here by the fire. You must be tired from your journey."

He turned his coal-black gaze toward her. His eyes were nearly black as midnight and framed in thick, dark lashes. But he did not respond and continued his survey of the room.

An audible sigh came from Sir Devlin's man.

"I could use a sit-down." Alden took a chair from the table and placed it closer to the fire. "And please excuse my tall, mute friend, my lady," he said as he sat down. "His manners are sorely lacking."

Rosalind did not reply, but the corners of her mouth turned up ever so slightly.

His friend is not afraid to goad him. Maybe that is a good sign.

A stressed silence filled the room, but thankfully, Ridley returned with a tray that held warm ale and cider. Marta also included chunks of cheese and a loaf of crusty bread in the late-night supper offering. Ridley walked to the head of the great table and plopped the tray down loudly.

Ridley moved toward his lady. Alden scooted his chair back to the table and began to drink the ale. Sir Devlin sat down, tore a chunk of the bread from the loaf, and ate, his quiet, intense stare focused on Rosalind.

Rosalind could not hold his piercing stare. She looked down and her wringing hands betrayed her.

Stop it!

Finally, she turned her head from his agonizing scrutiny. Her comfort obviously didn't concern him.

Out of the silence, his steady, serious voice said, "Do you know why I'm here?"

Rosalind's head turned upward and toward Sir Devlin. "Yes," she replied. "The king's missive was clear. You are looking for Lord Edmond, as he didn't arrive at court as expected." She was proud that her voice sounded strong.

"The king believes that his loyal vassal would never intentionally ignore a royal summons. I am here to discover whether foul play has kept him from attending to his liege or if he, by chance, turned traitorous. Anyone who interferes with my inquiry into this matter will be dealt with harshly. And if foul play is found to be the cause of his absence at court, anyone involved will be tried, judged, and sentenced accordingly."

Rosalind's heart pounded. She wondered if Sir Devlin could hear the beating.

His voice boomed, and he turned his cruel gaze toward all in the room. "And I expect—"

Benton, with an ancient grave voice, decided at this time to announce, "Your rooms are ready, Sir Devlin and Mr. Danby."

Rosalind stopped breathing; worried Benton would be punished for interrupting. But the dark menace paused and looked at the older servant for only a second before continuing.

"I will begin interviews first thing tomorrow. Are there any others who live here in the manor and are not present now?" Sir Devlin inquired.

"Just the children, Kaylyn and Luella. They are already abed upstairs."

"They will be included in the interviews. Am I

clear?" he said and turned to Rosalind.

She gave him a cursory nod, and then he and Alden turned and left the room, following Ridley to the stairs that adjoined the foyer just outside the main hall.

As soon as the men exited the room, Rosalind gasped. Marta ran from the kitchen and immediately attended to her.

"Deep breaths, milady," she said decisively and grabbed a chair. She forced Rosalind to sit, and she bent her head over to rest between her knees.

Panic had overtaken Rosalind, and she struggled to breathe. "Oh Marta, what are we to do? He already suspects us!"

"He can't prove anything!" Marta exclaimed. "Let him search and interview all he wants. If anything happened to that lecherous fool Edmond, it was probably his own fault!"

Rosalind's breathing calmed after several deep inhalations, and she sat up in her chair. "You're right, Marta. He'll find nothing."

But to her own ears, her words rang hollow.

Chapter Two

Thump! Ridley, who slept in a small room just off the pantry, woke to Marta's soft singing as she kneaded and punched the dough on the huge wooden table in the middle of the large kitchen. He sighed as he peeled back his covers on his bed. They were a warm cocoon that he didn't want to leave this cold winter morning. However, he had chores; the first was seeing to other's comfort before they awoke.

Keeping the large manor house running smoothly was an endeavor that required all who still resided there to work... and work hard. Each member of the household, whether servant or titled, had jobs to do. Marta always woke first, and she was busy in the kitchen long before the sun. Each morning, the smell of baking bread wafted through the great hall, up the stairs, and into the corridors that led to the bedrooms where the rest of the house still slept.

After dressing, he crept quietly upstairs, his single candle barely casting a shadow as he moved down the dark hall. He entered the bed chamber where his lady slept, stoked the fire with the heavy iron poker, and added a log. He then moved into the adjoining room where Kaylyn and little Luella slept and did the same. Normally this room would have been used as a sitting room for the lady of the house, reserved for reading or sewing, but Lady Rosalind preferred to house the girls there and keep them close. Ridley smiled when he heard Kaylyn snoring, and he'd be sure to tease her later.

Ridley didn't dawdle. Now that there were guests in the manor house, more fires needed tending.

Sir Devlin and Alden's quarters were next. Ridley moved quickly through the manor, his soft, thin soled shoes were silent on the rough stone floors. When he opened the door into Sir Devlin's chamber, the well-oiled, iron hinges on the heavy oak door made his entry silent, so he thought. He took two quiet steps into the room, but in an instant, the ice-cold edge of a dagger pressed at his throat.

"Sir! Sir Devlin, it is only I, Ridley! Please!" Ridley exclaimed.

"God's teeth! What do you think you are doing— sneaking in here? I could have killed you!" Devlin growled.

Devlin lowered the dagger, and walked back to his bed, muttering what Ridley was sure were expletives, something about dawn and how no one was up at this hour except thieves and mad men with a death wish.

"So sorry, sir. Milady prefers that I build up everyone's fires before they wake. The manor is quite drafty."

"Hrmmph," Devlin snorted, and he rolled back in bed.

Ridley moved to the fireplace and stirred the coals quickly. His hands shook when he picked up another log, and he dropped it to the floor. The wood thumped loudly on the stone hearth. A loud and very annoyed sigh erupted from Sir Devlin.

"Sorry, sir," he apologized again quietly.

A pillow flew from the bed and whacked him square in the face.

Ridley quickly picked up the log, completed his task, and left the room. Mr. Danby's room was directly across the hall, and this time he knocked and announced his presence. His only answer was Alden's enthusiastic snores that reverberated throughout the room. The large man never stirred while Ridley worked.

Finally, he came to Benton's small room at the end of the hall. Benton had served the Capell family for decades and had the privilege of a larger chamber. A small sliver of light broke through the wooden shutters, signaling the coming of the dawn, and Benton was still abed. Sometimes, the old servant woke as early as Marta, and he often sat and read in a comfortable chair by the fire—but not this morning. As Ridley crossed the room, he could just see Benton's body under the thick blankets on the bed. He looked very still.

"Benton," Ridley whispered. "Sir…"

Benton never moved.

"Benton. Sir," Ridley said again to see if Benton was awake.

Ridley stood for a moment. He crossed the room and grabbed a hand mirror hanging from a peg on the wardrobe. He carefully tiptoed back over to where Benton lay. He placed the edge of the mirror under Benton's nose and waited, holding his breath. Condensation appeared on the mirror.

He's alive! Ridley couldn't wait to tell Marta he had to do the mirror test on old Benton again this morning. Grinning, he completed his task at the fireplace and left the room. Back down in the kitchen, Ridley was eager to eat the breakfast Marta had prepared. Porridge and yesterday's bread with jam awaited him. The kitchen was warm and comfortable. Marta joined him at the table with a cup of tea, helped herself to a slice of bread, and added a generous dollop of the sweet fruit mixture. The early morning was their time to chat before the rest of the household rose.

"Sir Devlin nearly killed me," offered Ridley.

Marta's eyes widened and she choked a bit while sipping her tea.

"Just now, when I stoked his fire. I must have startled him when I entered the room."

Marta stared at him, unable to comment. "I never even heard him get out of bed, and I didn't see him move either. Like a dark, silent wolf waiting to pounce. No, not a wolf...worse than that—a hellhound he was. Couldn't see 'em, couldn't hear 'em. He was just...there. He could have slit my throat in a second." Ridley put another spoonful of porridge in his mouth.

"Oh dear sweet Father," Marta said as she crossed herself. "When Sir Devlin comes down, and you take the food out, you will apologize and ask him if he would rather you not enter his room in the morning. We cannot appear rattled, and we certainly do not want to rile this man."

Ridley's eyes widened. He frowned at the thought of talking to Sir Devlin, but he nodded in agreement.

"And I thought Benton was dead again this morning," Ridley stated matter-of-factly. "Had to use the mirror again."

"Ridley!" Marta exclaimed. "Don't be so flippant."

They ate in silence, but it wasn't long before the light thump of small feet was heard on the stairs, and young Luella ran down. She was a welcome distraction from the serious conversation that left the room quiet and heavy. Her honey-blond hair looked like a comb had never touched it, and her tunic dress was worn backward. Obviously, the child had not waited for Lady Rosalind or even her older sister to help her dress this morning. At four years of age, she wanted to do everything herself.

"Child! Where are your house slippers? You'll catch your death!" Marta chastised.

But no one could be cross with Luella, not for long anyway. Luella smiled, and her large brown eyes twinkled. She was a ray of sunshine in the room.

Marta, who was quite used to the little one appearing in disarray, grabbed a basket from the shelf next to the table and pulled out a comb.

"Come, little one, bring that tangled mess of hair here, and let's see what we can do."

Luella decided to comply with Marta's request and the cook began to work through the tangles carefully.

The pounding of larger feet was then heard on the stairs, and down came Kaylyn. She stomped rather unladylike towards Marta and Luella and, with a dramatic sigh, tossed her younger sibling's house slippers on the floor. Then, with a roll of her eyes, she went to the cookfire, spooned some porridge from the iron pot, and sat down to eat.

"Mama says your feet are going to freeze and fall off, you know." With a slight grin, Kaylyn directed this tidbit of information toward her younger sister.

Kaylyn, four years older than Luella, was cranky most mornings and not one to waste the sour attitude, she enjoyed aggravating her sibling.

The younger child replied, "That's not true!"

"Yes, it is," Kaylyn shot back.

"No, it's not!"

"It's true! Your feet will rot right off!"

And from there, the two girls argued back and forth. Ridley listened and grinned but did not join in the fray.

"Girls, girls! Stop the bickering. We have much to do today, and we have guests. You must be on your best behavior," Lady Rosalind implored as she entered the kitchen from the servants' staircase.

Dressed in a practical long-sleeve white linen chemise with a dark blue floor-length tunic, she wore a simple rope belt around her waist. In spite of Lord Edmond never allowing funds for fine dresses and accessories, Lady Rosalind looked beautiful. She wore her long chestnut brown hair in a tidy braid that trailed down her back, but curls escaped the braid at her temples and in front of her ears, framing her face. The dark circles under her eyes showed that Rosalind had not slept well at all last night. She filled a bowl with porridge and joined everyone at the table.

"Girls, I do not have the strength to endure such bickering this early in the morning. I barely slept a wink," she said as she took a bite of the warm porridge.

With eyes downcast, Kaylyn and Luella whispered in unison, "Sorry, Mama."

Rosalind looked up from her bowl and gave the girls a wan smile. The kitchen was quiet as everyone finished their breakfast. This morning the mood was quiet and filled with uncertainty and a feeling of dread.

The door that led from the kitchen to the great hall opened. Benton, looking unflappable as ever, entered the kitchen.

"Sir Devlin and Mr. Danby have taken their seats and look to break their fast," he announced.

Benton then walked to the sideboard and placed a pitcher of water on a tray, and Marta added a pitcher of warm cider. She placed two bowls, a small pot of porridge, a round of bread, and then jam. Then because they were guests, some dried fruit and cheese were added to the breakfast offering.

Ridley picked up the tray and followed Benton out to the table in the great hall.

****

Lady Rosalind took a deep breath, stood, and followed.

At the table, Rosalind's two guests sat, leaned in toward each other, and were speaking quietly. When they saw Ridley, followed by Benton, enter the room, they sat up quickly.

Ridley set the heavy tray on the end of the table, and Benton dutifully distributed the bowls, spoons, and cups between the men, then spooned out the porridge. The fruit and cheese were set out, and the pitchers were left for the men to serve themselves.

"Please send Ridley if you require anything else." With that, Benton started his painfully slow journey back to the kitchen.

Lady Rosalind stepped into the room, hesitant at first. Taking a deep breath, she gathered her composure and crossed to her chair by the fireplace, and sat. An awkward silence lingered before she spoke.

"Good morning, Sir Devlin, Mr. Danby. I trust you slept well."

"Yes, quite well," Alden replied.

"Hmmph," grumbled Devlin. "I was sleeping

comfortably until I was awoken before dawn by your Ridley there." He turned his scowl toward the boy.

Ridley's face turned a bit pale, and he took a step back. At the sight of Ridley's fear, Rosalind sat up straight, a flash of heat rose in her face, and she addressed Sir Devlin directly.

"Ridley was performing his morning duties as instructed by Lord Capell, and then by me, in his absence. He always stokes the fires before we wake. I, for one, enjoy waking up in a warm room. But if you prefer, he will leave your room cold," Rosalind stated firmly.

Cold like your black heart...

"Now that I know he comes each morning, I shall not be alarmed. I, too, prefer warmth over the damp and drafts of the stone walls."

Rosalind exhaled softly and slowly. She hadn't meant for her voice to sound so sharp. But no one, absolutely no one, was going to scare or threaten the children. Thankfully, in this instance, the dark man did not seem offended.

The men finished their morning meal quickly.

"I will speak to the children first this morning. You said there are two young girls who live here with you, correct? I will see them first and then Ridley."

"Is that really necessary?" Rosalind implored. "Luella is but four years old, and Kaylyn is only eight. I don't see what questions they would be able to answer."

It didn't seem possible for Sir Devlin's ever-constant frown to deepen, but it did.

"Do... not... question my commands, woman. I have orders directly from the king to question every person in this household. And that is what I shall do!"

Rosalind stood straight as if she had an iron spine. Then her chin lifted ever so slightly in defiance. Her left eyebrow rose as if in challenge. "Ridley, fetch the girls. They should be in the kitchen helping Marta. Bring them here," she said without ever taking her gaze off Sir Devlin. "As you wish... sir. But I will remain here in the room with them during your questioning." Her tone left no room for misunderstanding.

"That is fine. But you will not interfere with this interview."

She agreed with a slight nod of her head.

Alden cleared his throat. "I'll take my leave now. I will be questioning the surrounding tenant farmers to see what they know."

Alden gave Rosalind a slight bow and a nod to Devlin.

Rosalind had a feeling she knew what they had been discussing. They would inquire with the farmers, as it clearly wasn't enough to question Capell's family and servants.

Well, he's thorough...

Ridley returned with the two young girls in tow. Devlin held his hand out and motioned for them to take the two chairs across from him at the table.

"Ridley, see to saddling Mr. Danby's horse, and then see if Marta needs help in the kitchen. I will call on you when he is ready to speak with you," Rosalind said. "Girls, this is Sir Devlin. He's going to ask you some questions about Lord Edmond. Answer honestly. Sir Devlin, this is Kaylyn." She pointed to the child on his left. "And this is Luella," she added, indicating the child who sat to the right.

The two young girls sat across from their guest,

Kaylyn folded her hands, rested them on the table, and waited. Luella plopped into her seat with an indignant sigh and glanced at Rosalind and then back to Sir Devlin. Kaylyn had large, almond-shaped, dark brown eyes that looked both inquisitive and intelligent. Her near-black hair was pulled back in a flattering braid that fell down her back. Her frock was dusted with flour, and she sat ready and confident.

The younger of the two, Luella, looked more disheveled. Her honey-brown hair had already mostly escaped its braid and pins. Her brown eyes, which perfectly matched her sister's, looked angry.

"I heard you yell," little Luella stated matter-of-factly. "I heard you yell at Mama Rosalind. A gentleman doesn't yell at a lady," she admonished.

"Luella—" Rosalind began.

Devlin raised his hand. "No, she is right. But, young lady, what if I am not a gentleman? What then?"

"Mama says there's no excuse for bad behavior. And that means everyone. You need to 'pologize," Luella stated.

After a pause, Devlin sighed, "Lady Rosalind, please accept my apology for raising my voice earlier. I will strive not to let it happen again."

Lady Rosalind offered a slight grin, but looked toward Luella. "I accept your apology. Now then, Luella, let Sir Devlin ask his questions."

The girls nodded, and Devlin began. "Do either of you know where Lord Edmond is?"

Both girls shook their heads no.

"Do either of you remember the last day that he was here?"

Kaylyn nodded. "Yes, I remember. He was here in

the great hall, and he had drunk too much ale. He was drunk nearly all the time. He yelled at Mama about not having enough money. Said it was her fault. He started getting mean. We could hear him yelling from the kitchen."

"How was he mean?" Devlin asked.

"Where did you get that mark? That mark on your face?" Luella interrupted.

"I was cut in a sword fight."

Luella sighed.

"Were you fighting a pirate? I bet he was fighting a pirate, Luella," Kaylyn chimed in.

"A pirate!" Luella yelled.

"It was not a fight with a pirate," Devlin said. "It was a fight with a man who was an enemy of England."

"Your eye… it could have been plucked right out!" Luella exclaimed. "Mama always tells us to be very careful when we sword fight with Ridley. Were you careful, Mr. Devil?"

"It's Devlin, Sir Devlin," he corrected. "And what are you doing playing with swords, anyhow?"

"Just wooden swords," Luella said. "And did you poke the other man? Did he lose his eye?"

"Yes, just a little bit higher, and your eye would have gone rolling across the ground," Kaylyn offered with a bit too much gory enthusiasm.

"Just like the ball Benton made Ridley!"

Luella laughed and made a fist with her hand, pretending that her fist popped out of her eye and bounced off the table onto the ground. Kaylyn jumped up and joined the hilarity, adding some realistic eye-popping sounds.

"Girls! That is enough! Please listen to Sir Devlin,"

Rosalind ordered harshly.

But inside, she chuckled. She knew how conversations with the girls could quickly go downhill. She glanced at Sir Devlin. He leaned back in his chair and had a look of sheer defeat on his face.

"Pray, continue, Sir Devlin," she said more calmly.

"How was Lord Capell mean, Kaylyn?" Kaylyn looked at Rosalind before she spoke. "When he drank too much, he yelled really loud and he would call Mama Rose bad names. And Ridley. And us, too. That's what he was doing. Saying bad things that we aren't ever supposed to say."

"Words like bastard," Kaylyn said.

"And whore," Luella added. With her hand cupped around her mouth, she whispered, "And ass!"

Kaylyn began to add to the list. "Turd…"

"Bloody whoreson…"

"Girls! That is enough!" Rosalind interjected. "Oh, what must Sir Devlin think of you!"

"Did you see Lord Edmond anymore after that night when he was yelling?"

Both girls said they hadn't.

"That's all the questions I have for you both at this time," he said, his shoulders slumped and his brow pinched. He looked between each girl and then shook his head slightly.

"Kaylyn, Luella, return to the kitchen and help Marta. I will be there shortly to fetch Ridley when Sir Devlin is ready. He looks as if he may need a little break from questioning."

The girls rose from the table, and Kaylyn left the room.

But Luella ran to Sir Devlin and gave him a quick

hug. She looked at him with her big brown eyes and said seriously, "Lord Edmond scared me." She paused, and then said, "Every day."

Devlin's arms hung limply at his sides at first, but then he managed to give the little girl a small squeeze. Luella ran to the kitchen.

"I've questioned killers for hire, traitors, and hardened warriors, and I feel that none of my past experiences prepared me well enough to question those two!"

Rosalind nodded in understanding. "The girls are very… imaginative and, shall I say, spirited. But they simply had no information to give, Sir Devlin. To be honest, I sheltered the girls from Lord Edmond as much as possible. They had very little contact with him, But what Kaylyn said is very true, unfortunately. Lord Edmond indulged in drinking too much on more days than not. He was always cruel, but when he was drunk, his mood was quite dangerous. I never wanted the girls to witness or, worse, be the focus of his anger."

"You didn't birth either child, did you? Kaylyn is eight, so you would have been too young. Who were their parents? Are they Lord Edmond's bastards?"

Chapter Three

Lady Rosalind moved from the table and sat in her rocking chair by the great fireplace. She picked up her mending basket and pulled out a pair of gray woolen stockings with holes in the feet. From the basket, she procured two knitting needles and a ball of woolen yarn. She inhaled a deep breath.

"My parents died in a carriage accident when I was ten years old. My mother had no family, and Lord Edmond was my father's only surviving relation, so the king awarded Uncle Edmond guardianship over me. When I came to live here, I was scared and alone, and it didn't take much time for me to realize that Lord Edmond held no affection for me at all. Rather, he was only interested in the modest monthly stipend he received from monies collected from my father's estate."

As Devlin listened, he related to Rosalind's story, which in some ways was much like his own.

"Marta and Benton immediately took me in and loved me as much as any parent would. Years ago, before my uncle ran off all the servants, Marta had help in the kitchen; a young girl named Agnes. She was about thirteen or fourteen years old. From nearly day one, we were inseparable. I had always wanted a sister."

Devlin noticed a slight smile on Rosalind's face as

she reminisced. She dropped a stitch in her knitting and didn't continue until she had picked it back up on her knitting needle.

"A few years later, Agnes married a young man who lived nearby, but she continued to work here in the manor. It wasn't long before Kaylyn was born, and then little Luella four years later. Agnes was so happy upon finding herself pregnant again. She was blessed with Kaylyn but didn't want her growing up as an only child."

"It seems you were all a happy family," Devlin said.

"We were. But Lord Edmond's drinking got worse, and Agnes caught his eye. His unwanted advances became commonplace, and one day, her husband, Tom, walked into the kitchen and Agnes was trying to ward off Edmond's unwelcome attention."

"I understand this didn't end well?" Devlin inquired and tears welled up in Rosalind's eyes. She worked another stitch into the foot of the stocking in her hand.

"No, not at all. An altercation broke out, and Edmond was left bloodied on the kitchen floor. Tom fled, knowing that he would be punished and jailed, and he was never seen again."

Devlin still waited patiently for the answer to his question.

"I know what you are thinking. But the girls were Tom's, Sir Devlin. No question about that."

"So where is Agnes now?"

Did Edmond have her tucked away somewhere? Did he have her jailed?

"Agnes was broken-hearted after Tom's

disappearance. She held out hope that he had gotten away. But after several weeks and no sign or word from him, she wondered if he was actually dead."

"What do you think? Do you think he got away?" Devlin asked softly.

"No. I think Edmond had him killed. He would not stand for an underling to insult him in such a way."

Rosalind's voice grew softer, and the sadness in her eyes was evident. "Three months later, Agnes became ill. We did all we could, but the fever took her life."

Rosalind was quiet for a moment. "She made me promise to raise her girls... and keep them safe. I've kept my promise. The girls are mine now."

After a brief but heavy silence, the sadness in her face was replaced with resolve. She added, "And I'll do whatever it takes to keep them safe."

Devlin didn't doubt for a moment that she would.

Rosalind cleared her throat and stood from her chair. She carefully folded her mending and placed it back in the basket. "Are you ready for Ridley now? I think you'll find him a bit more manageable."

Devlin nodded, and Rosalind left the dining hall to fetch Ridley.

****

Rosalind entered the kitchen through the swinging door. Marta sat by the kitchen hearth, peeling carrots. Marta appeared to be concentrating on her work, but Rosalind knew the expression on her face was one of concerned curiosity.

"Kaylyn... Luella... how did they fare being questioned by that black devil?" Marta stood quickly and asked worriedly, "Was he cruel? Did he scare them?"

Rosalind placed her hands on Marta's plump arms. "They were fine. They are fine, Marta. The girls were not intimidated at all."

Marta sat back down and sighed in relief. Her tense expression disappeared and a small smile tugged at her edges of her mouth.

"Answered prayers!" she announced. "I couldn't bear for the little ones to be frightened more than they are day to day here."

Rosalind nodded. "I had concerns too, but Marta, I think there is more to this man than we know. When he questioned the girls, he was calm. His voice was almost soothing. I think the girls trusted him right away."

Marta blinked once and then stared wide-eyed at Rosalind in disbelief.

"Yes, it's true. And since they trusted him, the conversation got away from him. But you know what? He never lost his patience. Not once!"

Marta looked heavenward. "Perhaps we have misjudged this man then, milady."

Rosalind hoped so, and then she sent up a silent prayer that Sir Devlin would be their advocate and not their adversary in the days to come.

****

A few short minutes later, Ridley raced around the corner and plopped himself in the chair across from Devlin.

Devlin looked at the lad sitting in front of him. His homespun trousers and oversized linen shirt swallowed his slight frame. Devlin noted that despite being a servant, he wore shoes, which was unusual for a child of his station. His hair was clean, but too long, and the child had a way of flipping his head to the side to get the longer tresses out of his eyes. His face and hands were clean, but there was dirt under his fingernails.

"So, Ridley. Were you in the manor house the night Lord Edmond was last seen?"

"Yes, sir. Yes, I was."

"Tell me what you saw and heard that night."

"That night, I helped Marta in the kitchen like I always do. I fetched water and kept the cooking fires hot. Marta had fixed chicken stew—it's very good—one of my favorite things she cooks." Ridley smiled. "I had already carried out the bread and bowls and such, but when I took the soup pot out to Benton to serve, Lord Edmond was already deep in his cups and swearin' and carrying on."

"What did he say?" Devlin asked.

"Something about not having enough money and how taking care of milady and her 'two brats' was breaking him. He told her he'd found a way to recover his losses."

"What do you think he meant by that, Ridley?" Devlin sensed he was getting somewhere.

"I… don't know," Ridley said hesitantly.

But Devlin was sure Ridley lied. "What did Lady Rosalind say in response?"

"Milady. She's no mouse, you know. She stood right up and called him a drunk sot and told him he'd have plenty of money if he didn't drink so much and piss it right in the chamber pot," Ridley said proudly.

"I don't guess Lord Edmond took this well?"

"He sure didn't. He reached right across the table and slapped her hard across the face. I got so angry. I started to reach for a knife, I did, but Benton said he would handle it and pushed me toward the kitchen. He said to get Kaylyn and Luella and go hide and not to come back until Benton said it was all right to do so."

"What did you do?"

Ridley's eyes grew wider and his freckles stood out in sharp contrast to his pale face. "I ran to the kitchen and told the girls we had to hide. And that's what we did. We hid. We hid until Benton said it was safe to come out."

"And when was this?" Devlin asked.

"It was late. The girls and I had fallen asleep. Benton came and woke us, and we went straight to our rooms and crawled in bed."

"Did you have to take the girls and hide very often, Ridley?"

"More often than I'd like. But we had the perfect hiding spot. We only had to wait until the old lord passed out, and then it was safe to come out," he explained matter-of-factly. "I only wish milady would have hidden with us."

"And what of Lady Rosalind? Did you see her before you went to your room?"

"No, no, I didn't. The girls sleep upstairs, and I sleep down here in a room off the kitchen. She wasn't in the kitchen or great hall when I went down, but she was up in her chamber, I'm sure."

Devlin thought for a moment and began to see a clearer picture of what life was like here at Capell Manor—and it was not a pleasing picture at all.

"Ridley, that will be all. You can return to your chores."

It seemed to Devlin that Lord Edmond was losing money and turned his angst toward Lady Rosalind. His blood boiled at the thought of Rosalind being struck by her guardian. But what did he mean when he said she would have to earn her keep? Titled ladies did not work, not as servants, nannies, or anything else; that would be scandalous.

But the children were orphans. They lived here only because the lord had allowed it, so why did he? So far he had learned nothing of Edmond's character that would suggest he would support two orphaned peasant children.

There was much to think about, but Ridley appeared and told him Mr. Danby had arrived back and was unsaddling his horse in the stable.

Oh good. Maybe Alden learned more than I have today.

Benton met him with his cloak at the door. Devlin donned the garment and walked out into the brisk, damp air.

The sun was shining, but its rays did little to cast warmth into his body. He looked at the manor house that once stood proud but now looked tired and neglected. Edmond didn't spend money on the upkeep of his home, that much was certain.

The sprawling manor consisted of two levels and then a third-level attic space that at one time would have housed servants. Brown vines crept up the weathered stone walls and into the cracks where the stone crumbled away. Perhaps in the summer, when the vines were green and full, they hid the crevices and faults in the masonry. Capell Manor boasted several glass windows, and those on the main floors were clean and clear, but those on the third were covered with grime, and one was broken.

Then his gaze panned left and right, and he assessed Edmond's lands. The fields were level to rolling, and a forest of hardwoods bordered the estate to the north. There was potential here for a prosperous estate. If he needed money, why had Edmond never cultivated the land?

A well-worn path led to the stable. Young Ridley wrestled a large saddle off Alden's horse.

Alden stepped up to help the boy, but he muttered, "I've got it." And just as he appeared to topple with the weight of the gear, he righted himself and dragged the saddle over to a rack, placing it there. He returned to the horse and began brushing its white hide with a soft brush.

"The boy has a way with the horses," Alden said as Devlin approached.

"Young Ridley seems to be a hard worker," Devlin acknowledged. "But grooming doesn't prove he's a good horseman."

Alden shrugged. "Maybe, maybe not. But that demon of a horse of yours enjoyed a good groom and several treats just before you walked up."

Devlin stared in disbelief at his friend, but he didn't come out to speak about Ridley or horses for that matter. "Tell me. Did you find anything useful?" he questioned with a clipped tone.

"Not much," Alden replied.

Devlin's eyes narrowed, his mouth set into a line. His jaw flexed.

"I questioned every farmer that worked lands within an hour's ride from the manor. There weren't many," he noted.

"None of them had anything good to say about

Edmond. One was even so bold as to tell me to check the nearest brothel or even the pits of hell, and that's where we would find him. But none had seen him or offered up any useful information."

Devlin emitted a long, frustrated sigh.

"Except for one." Devlin's interest was piqued again.

"One man, who lives directly east of here, said that Lord Edmond's mount was found outside his cottage, quietly eating hay the morning after he supposedly went missing."

"Did he see any signs of Edmond?" Devlin asked.

"He said he fetched his son from his bed and told him to take the horse back to the manor house immediately and inform Lady Rosalind of finding the horse the way they did—saddled but no rider."

Devlin's temper flared. No one mentioned that Edmond's horse was found, saddled, the day after his disappearance.

"He then jumped on his old nag and went looking for Edmond. He figured he'd gotten drunk and taken a fall from his horse. He said he rode for nearly an hour, but there was no sign of him. "But here is something strange." Alden paused. "When the son returned the horse to the manor, he was met by Benton at the servant's entrance. The boy told him that he had an important message concerning Lord Edmond for the lady."

"There's nothing odd about that," scoffed Devlin. "For your sake, I hope there is more to this telling than you've disclosed so far, friend."

Alden gave a slight nod of agreement and continued. "I found out that Benton, yes, the ancient relic of a manservant, told the boy that he would hear his message and that Lady Rosalind was not to be told or bothered as she might find the news upsetting. The farmer said his son was intimidated by the normally mild-mannered servant's tone. So, the boy told Benton about the horse he had put in the stables, and he left."

Devlin thought for a moment, and he wondered why Benton was withholding information from his lady. It seemed improbable that the old man had something to do with the disappearance, but he wasn't going to rule the possibility out.

"Interesting…" muttered Devlin, but he didn't elaborate on his thoughts.

"What about you? Did you uncover anything in your interviews this morning?" Alden inquired.

"Nothing of real substance. I've only spoken to the children. But I learned that Lady Rosalind and Lord Edmond had an argument, and Edmond struck his niece across the table. And that Edmond often behaved that way. Ridley and the girls often hid in a secret location until Edmond passed out and it was safe to exit again."

Alden shook his head in disgust. "Lord Edmond sounds like a real gentleman."

Devlin watched as the boy eased his head out of the stall and eavesdropped on the men's conversation, a pitchfork still in his hand.

"You have something to add, boy?" Devlin called out. "Did you know about the horse being found and returned the day after Edmond left the manor?"

Ridley slipped back into the stall as if he didn't hear the question, so Devlin and Alden walked over to the door and peered between the wooden slats.

"Answer my question, Ridley," Devlin

commanded.

Ridley stopped his work, turned to the men, "Yes, I did. But not until later that evening. I overheard Benton tell Lady Rosalind."

"And what was the lady's reaction to that news?" Alden asked.

"I wasn't able to hear all of what she said. But she wondered if he was attacked by a highwayman. Something like that."

"And that's all you heard?" Devlin pressed further.

Ridley nodded, and as he left the stall, he replied, "Yes, that's all I heard. Now, I must finish here. Marta gets quite cross if I spend too much time with the horses, and I still have work to do."

"'Ey! Mr. Dandy! Where's the hound?"

Devlin gave Alden a questioning glance. "Did you bring Grim back with you from the fields?"

"I did. He went to your horse's stall as he usually does. I'll take a look around and see if I can find him. Probably ventured out and found a rabbit to chase."

"See that you find him," Devlin commanded. "Ridley, come with me. We will look on our way back to the house."

They both scanned the lands to each side of them. After only a moment, Marta screamed, along with the sound of a loud crash coming from the kitchen. Sir Devlin and Ridley sprinted to the door and leaped inside.

"What is it, woman?" Devlin asked quickly.

A large goose stuffed for the evening meal lay on the floor, and potatoes, parsnips, and carrots were strewn across the kitchen.

Marta's hands shook, but he quickly realized she

was more angry than frightened.

"Who let that devil dog of yours out of the stable?!" she yelled. "Look at our dinner!" She pointed at the floor.

Marta then grabbed a large iron pan from a hook hanging from the ceiling and shook it in the air. Devlin was impressed, and a bit frightened himself. That pan must have weighed as much as a small child, but she swung it easily.

"Where did he go?" she bellowed fiercely, and she started in the direction of where the dog ran. "I'll teach him, I will!"

Devlin ran after Marta, her bum leg not troubling her a bit now, he observed. Ridley was not far behind. But when they reached the great hall, the scene that met them brought them all to a standstill.

Grim, the fierce, warrior dog who fought alongside his master, the dog that shredded the arms and legs of many men, and struck fear in all who saw him with Sir Devlin, was approaching Rosalind and the children.

Devlin's heart jumped in his throat. Grim had never met a child. He never allowed anyone to touch him except for Devlin and sometimes Alden. The dog trusted no one.

Lady Rosalind sat in her chair with her mending but had heard the commotion in the kitchen. She looked toward Devlin and Marta, and then her gaze traveled to the side of the room where she saw the large black dog walking, or perhaps stalking, in her direction.

"Don't move, Rosalind. Children, for God's sake, just sit still. I will get the dog."

Alden appeared next to Devlin and gasped.

"Alden, ready your sword," Devlin said with a

catch in his voice.

Rosalind looked at them all like each of them had grown an extra head. "Why do you all look so frightened?" she asked innocently.

By this time, Grim had sauntered over to Rosalind's chair. The dog didn't appear to be bristling or showing signs of aggression, but still, Devlin stood frozen. He didn't want to make any sudden movements. Grim's massive head almost held level with Rosalind's face. She placed her mending in her lap and focused her attention on the massive beast now standing next to her chair.

"Aren't you magnificent?"

Grim's ears flicked forward, and his yellow eyes fixed on Rosalind.

Rosalind's hand reached out.

Chapter Four

"Stop, don't! He'll..." Devlin called to her.

But it was too late. The gentle lady had already begun to give Grim a thorough ear scratch while simultaneously cooing and praising him for his handsomeness and loyalty to his master. Devlin could not believe his eyes. The beast of a dog sat at Lady Rosalind's feet and leaned his massive head into her hand. After a moment, Grim lay down, and Rosalind continued the scratching, except this time on his exposed belly.

Alden moved closer to Devlin, and he dropped his bow and sheathed his sword. "Your warrior dog...he's ruined now," Alden stated with some degree of annoyance. "That perfectly honed weapon of death has turned soft in only a moment with the touch of a woman."

Devlin was speechless. Did Grim enjoy this affection? Could he be trusted to be gentle with the lady, or would he snap without warning or provocation? Then Luella and Kaylyn approached the dog.

Grim had never been in the company of children. Devlin sprinted toward the girls.

But he was too late. Luella and Kaylyn had dropped to their knees, and now Grim had four smaller hands rubbing his belly, and all three of the females in the room were telling him what a good boy he was and how he was strong and brave.

What witchcraft is this?

No one but he and Alden were able to touch Grim. And when they did, it was never with affection.

"What...are..." Devlin sputtered. "What are you doing to my dog? He's dangerous...please be careful...stop!" Devlin yelled the last word of his plea.

"Sir Devlin, what are you going on about? Your hound obviously enjoys the attention from the girls and me to your heavy-handed care. We are just fine," Rosalind said. "Now, if you have anything to discuss, I suggest we sit for our midday meal, and we can engage in conversation there if you so please."

Devlin felt as if the tables had turned in the space of just one morning. Last night he had gone to bed thinking that the cook was weak and could hardly walk, the lady of the manor was timid and meek, the old manservant was feeble and slow-witted, the young girls were frightened little mice, and the kitchen boy was unintelligent.

But now he looked around the room and saw that the cook was ready to take on a ferocious dog with a frying pan, the lady of the manor and the children were fearless, and the manservant and the kitchen boy were quite clever and possibly hiding a serious misdeed or even worse-a murder.

Devlin sat down in the chair closest to him. "Ridley!" he bellowed. "Bring me some ale."

Ridley ran to the kitchen with Marta following right on his heels.

Bum leg, my arse!

Benton, who had arrived late to the scene, looked at Rosalind, the girls, and the dog, shook his head, and announced to the room, "I will return with the meal. my lady, Kaylyn and Luella, you may want to wash a bit after your enthusiastic attention to the killer hellhound."

Devlin rolled his eyes. The children and Lady Rosalind rose and strolled toward the kitchen.

"And you, Grim," Benton said with authority. "You may rest here in the hall as long as you present yourself with impeccable manners during your stay."

Grim's ears perked up, and he looked at the servant with his head tilted to the side.

Then Benton tottered over to the large wooden chest that sat left of the fireplace. He opened the lid and took out a large woolen blanket. He unfolded the blanket halfway and laid it in front of the fire. Grim stood until his bed was ready. Then he dropped clumsily to the pallet, his head resting between his paws.

Devlin's head ached.

The girls returned with their non-stop chatter. Ridley followed with a tray of food and Marta was behind him with mugs of ale.

Lady Rosalind sat at the head of the table, and the girls assisted Benton in ladling the stew into the trenchers. The girls weren't much help for old Benton, more stew was spilled than made it into the bowls, but Devlin had to admit that the food smelled delicious. Marta added two round loaves of rich brown bread to the table and then called Ridley and the girls.

"Come, children, I have your bowls in the kitchen."

The children left amicably, and the room suddenly silent. Alden dove into his meal with enthusiasm, and with each bite placed in his mouth, he emitted a content sigh.

"Will you stop doing that?" Devlin scolded.

Lady Rosalind came to his defense. "Nothing wrong with showing your appreciation for a warm meal on a cold day, is there, Mr. Danby?"

"I agree wholeheartedly, but he can keep his groanings to himself." Devlin snapped back.

Alden gave Lady Rosalind a quick wink, and the action was not unnoticed by Devlin.

"So, Mr. Danby, did your questioning of the tenant farmers and villagers provide any insights into our mystery?" Lady Rosalind asked curiously.

"We were able to find out that Lord Edmond's horse was returned here to the manor the morning after he disappeared. A farmer by the name of Henry woke to find the animal eating hay with his goats early that morning."

Rosalind's face paled.

Alden continued, "Henry secured the horse, then saddled his own nag and looked for Edmond. He figured the Lord had been thrown from the horse and was lying injured somewhere. But his search yielded nothing."

Devlin turned to Rosalind. "Did you know Capell's horse had been found?"

Rosalind swallowed, "Yes. Yes...of course, I did." With a barely noticeable tremble in her voice, she said, "And we sent out our own search parties immediately after we discovered the horse was found riderless." Her hand shook slightly as she made a feeble attempt at eating her meal, and her gaze was fixed on the trencher in front of her.

"And you searched the lands around the manor thoroughly?" Devlin asked.

"Yes, we did. As best as a ninety-year-old servant and I could. We didn't get much help from the village, either."

Devlin thought her point was a good one. A lady and ancient Benton could not search the surrounding farmland thoroughly. And seeing that Lord Capell wasn't well-liked, he didn't doubt that the villagers were less than enthusiastic about helping.

"So, where do you go from here?" Rosalind asked.

"I still need to interview Benton and Marta. I plan on doing that now," Devlin replied.

Rosalind nodded and then stood. "I have to start the children's lessons. Please excuse me," she said curtly as she gathered her mug and trencher.

The men waited until she left the room, and Alden shook his head, "I do not think our lady is telling us all she knows."

Devlin looked down the hall. "I agree, Alden. I agree."

After completing their meal, mostly in silence, Benton appeared with Ridley tagging along. The man and boy cleared the table.

"I'd like to speak to you, Benton. Right away," Devlin said, using a tone that left no question that he would tolerate anything other than immediate compliance.

"Certainly, sir," Benton replied. "Let me return the tray to the kitchen, and I will return post haste."

Each step was painfully slow. But Devlin also noticed the loving respect Ridley showed Benton. He carried the water pitchers so that Benton's tray was not overly heavy. And he didn't run ahead. He walked with Benton and never seemed to mind his snail's pace.

"You've got time for a lie-down before he gets back," Alden jested.

Not in the mood for jokes, Devlin's scowl was fierce, but he did not offer to comment.

"Grim will make room for you by the fire."

A frustrated grunt escaped from Devlin, but he was now alone in the great hall. His mind worked to deduce who was the most likely suspect in Lord Capell's demise. Yes, the discovery of his horse, saddled and no rider, led him to conclude that the lord had most likely died. But was it foul play or an accident? Even if he were thrown from his horse, he would have died from the elements by now, and wild animals would have taken his remains. However, considering that Henry had made a search and another by her ladyship and her servant, he was more inclined to believe foul play was involved. And if there was a crime, it was not committed by common thieves. Ruffians would have taken the fine saddle, bridle, and the horse itself.

Devlin heard the soft shuffle of feet and looked up to see Benton entering the room.

"Send Ridley to the stables if he is free from duties this afternoon," Alden said as he stood to leave. "I have some repairs to my saddle that I need done. The boy can help."

Devlin nodded, and Alden left the room. Benton made his way to the table. He motioned for the butler to sit, and the old man sat gingerly in the chair across from Devlin.

For a moment, the two men looked at each other. The only sounds heard in the room were the occasional crackle of the fire and Grim's soft snores.

"Benton," Devlin finally began. "Were you witness

to the tense exchange that occurred between Lord Capell and Lady Rosalind the last night he was seen?"

"Yes, sir. I was in the dining room when the altercation began," he replied.

"And what did you believe your Lord was angry about?"

"Oh, he was enraged about what he was usually angry about, Sir Devlin. He was furious about the state of his finances, or lack thereof, I should say."

"Didn't Capell bring in enough money from the rents of his lands?"

"Lord Edmond collected the rents each year, as he should have. He also received funds from Lady Rosalind's estate. But he was not wise in managing his funds."

Benton's face flushed with emotion. Devlin could not tell if it was from anger or maybe it was sadness.

Benton continued, "This lord squandered every shilling he had on drink and whoring. And what he had left, he gambled away. I served his father, and my father served this family two generations before that. The Capell name was respected once. But no more!"

"Yes, I gather from the questioning Alden conducted in the village and the farms that no one held him in high esteem."

"And the way he treated his only relation. Lady Rosalind was more of a servant here than his niece and heir. A disgrace, I tell you!"

Devlin hadn't thought about Rosalind's value. Value in that she would inherit not only her father's lands but also Capell's.

Devlin wondered if the king had planned to use Rosalind to bolster allegiance from the border lords through a marriage contract. "Who was to decide on Lady Rosalind's future husband? Lord Edmond or King Charles?"

"I understood that the king would allow Lord Edmond to choose her husband, but he would not turn loose of her estate unless the future groom agreed to continue the work Edmond does to ferret out and report any suspicious activity to the king directly. The king fears that the Parliamentarian movement will gain in popularity, and he wants to know which of his lords and citizens would support a rebellion," Benton said.

"So, the king wishes to strengthen his alliances along the border of Wales," Devlin said more to himself than Benton.

But none of this was particularly nefarious. Marriages were arranged all the time. It was a woman's duty to secure her family's future or benefit her country with a sound marriage arrangement.

Devlin thought for a moment, "But what of the children? Ridley said Capell had found a way to recover his losses concerning Luella and Kaylyn as well. What did he mean?"

Benton lowered his gaze for a second, but when he raised his head, he looked Devlin right in the eye. "I was not privy to Lord Edmond's plans for the girls. But I do know that many of his acquaintances were some of the most unsavory of characters with the blackest of hearts. I have no doubt that our girls could have ended up leaving with any one of the degenerates he often associated with." Benton's eyes teared up.

Was this the type of man the king relied on? Did King Charles know the depravity of Lord Edmond's character? Or maybe the king did not care. His main concern was protecting the absolute power of the monarchy.

Devlin was afraid of what Benton would reply, but he asked, "Did Edmond abuse the children?"

"He tried, Sir Devlin. The children often raised his ire. But Lady Rosalind never allowed him to harm them. She kept them out of his sight as much as possible, but sometimes that wasn't enough. She would then become the object of his anger and suffer for it."

Devlin thought of Rosalind. Her devotion to the children and her obvious love and care for the servants was unlike anything he'd ever seen or experienced. Her affection and fondness for the entire household was not something seen amongst the nobility. Devlin thought about how fortunate she was to have found a family, though unconventional, that obviously adored and loved her in return after being sent to live with her rotter of an uncle.

Devlin steered the discussion back to the beginning. "Let's return back to the night in question, the last night Edmond was seen. What happened after Capell struck Lady Rosalind? Did she fight back?"

"The argument became very heated," Benton said. "Lord Edmond told her she would soon be gone, and his troubles would be over."

Devlin leaned in, "Go on. What did she say?"

"She told him that she would never marry any of the churlish swine that he wanted to sell her off to. She then left the hall and ran to her chamber."

"Did Capell follow?"

"No. He downed his goblet of wine and yelled for another. I gave him another and then left," Benton answered. "Usually, when he was in that dangerous of a mood, he went to the village for more drinking and to find a whore, willing or unwilling."

"Did you hear Capell come back to the manor that evening?" Devlin prodded.

Benton shook his head, "No, but that wasn't unusual. He often stayed out all night."

"Did you see anyone else leave the manor after the argument?" Devlin stared into Benton's rheumy eyes. "Answer carefully."

Benton paused. "No, I did not see anyone leave the manor."

Devlin sat back in his chair and sighed, "Thank you, Benton. I don't have any other questions. Could you please ask Marta to come here? I'd like to question her now."

"Very well, sir." Benton rose from the table and again began his trek back to the kitchen.

As the flames from the fire danced in the hearth, he realized that everyone in the manor had the motive to see Lord Capell dead. But it was unfathomable to him that anyone here could actually accomplish the deed. The risks were too high. His thoughts were interrupted as Marta entered. He motioned for her to sit down.

Devlin didn't need to hear any more about how much of a louse Capell was, so he thought he would get to the point with his questions for the cook. "Marta. Did you hear the argument or see the altercation between your lady and Lord Capell on the night he was last seen?"

"Oh, no, sir," she replied quickly. "I was in the kitchen and I didn't even know there was anything going on until Ridley ran in and got the girls and said they needed to hide. I then knew something had happened. I made sure the children got up the stairs, and then I peeked around the corner."

"What did you see?" Devlin hoped to glean some new information.

"I saw Lady Rosalind running from the room. Lord Capell sat for just a moment, downed his wine, and threw the goblet to the ground. He yelled for more. I made sure he didn't see me."

"Did you see Lord Edmond after that? Even later in the evening or through the night?" Devlin asked, but he knew the answer.

"No sir, no, I didn't."

Frustrated, Devlin waved his hand, dismissing her with a long sigh. There was only Lady Rosalind to question now. He left to seek her out.

Grim, feeling rested after his nap by the fire, joined him as he searched for the lady of the house. She had said she would be conducting the children's lessons. After finding no one in two of the downstairs rooms, he finally heard voices in the stairwell, and laughter. Grim was attracted to the sound, and he led Devlin up the steps and down the hall to a solarium.

Moving quietly, he approached the open door and peered inside. The room boasted several large windows that surprisingly held glass instead of being covered with wooden shutters. Warm sunlight filtered through each one, casting swathes of light throughout the room.

A fireplace helped keep the chill from the room, and a comfortable woolen rug, dyed red, sat at the edge of the hearth. In the middle of the chamber, a sturdy wooden table stood with six chairs around its perimeter. Two additional tall-back chairs rested against the far wall, and a settee was positioned in front of the fire.

The room was warm and comfortable. It was obvious Lady Rosalind and the children spent much of their time here. A basket of blocks, a collection of homemade dolls, and a sewing box with threads and unfinished embroidery pieces rested by the settee that was near the fire.

Devlin never had any such comforts growing up. These children were fortunate that the lady of the manor sought to make this house a home. His thoughts were interrupted with a low moan, and he looked around to see Ridley at the table with his head in his hands.

"Why do I need to learn to read? No one of my lot learns to read," he lamented.

Devlin smiled. He remembered many such lessons growing up. His father had insisted on an education for his only son, but he had not been a willing participant.

"Mama says if you don't learn to read, you'll grow up to be the village idiot," Kaylyn chided.

Little Luella nodded her head in agreement.

"Girls, that's not what I said. Just because someone can't read doesn't make them any less intelligent than any other person. But knowing how to read can make you smarter," Rosalind explained patiently. "Ridley, you could become a merchant, a clerk, or even a great architect. You don't have to work in the kitchen all your life."

At that, Ridley rolled his eyes, but he focused on the slate tablet in front of him, "I'd rather raise horses, milady."

Grim made his entrance, and both girls squealed in delight. The fierce dog wasted no time, only traveled about three feet and he clumsily plopped down on the sun-warmed floor, leaving his underbelly exposed to the bright rays of light and the tender scratches from the girls. Devlin shook his head.

"Yes, Sir Devlin. What can I assist you with?" If she was perturbed at the interruption, she didn't show any outward signs.

At her question, Devlin turned and looked at Rosalind. Long black eyelashes framed her large brown eyes, and a curly tendril of hair had escaped her braid. She had a smudge of the powdery rock residue she used to scratch letters onto Ridley's tablet on her cheek.

"Sir Devlin," she repeated.

He broke his gaze. "I need…" his voice practically squeaked. He cleared his throat, "I need to complete your questioning. But I see that you are occupied. Perhaps you can grant me an audience tomorrow?"

"Yes, that will be fine. I want to complete Ridley's reading lesson. The girls finish more quickly as they are more willing pupils, but they need to work on their stitching."

The girls ran to a basket beside the settee and pulled out pieces of fabric that were stretched upon a small frame. Threads of different colors hung from the back of the fabric.

Kaylyn reached him first. "Look, Sir Devlin. Mama says my stitches are improving."

Devlin didn't really know what to say. Women and sewing were not anything he knew or even cared about. But he wasn't a complete ogre so he took the frame from her hands and looked at her work.

On the fabric, he could see she practiced many different stitches. He saw clearly her shaky, uneven, first attempts and how she improved as more were completed. In one corner he saw a blue flower that wasn't quite finished.

"This...this is very good," he said hesitantly but sincerely.

Kaylyn was satisfied with his praise, and she gifted him with a big smile. She took her work and sat on the settee.

"Now me, sir! Look at mine!" Luella nearly jumped with excitement.

Devlin took her smaller sewing frame. Her stitches were terribly uneven, but considering her young age, he deemed them not bad at all.

"Your work is very good too, Luella. You'll be sewing the finest of dresses and creating bold tapestries for the king before you know it."

Luella giggled. "I'd rather be a faerie, Sir Devlin, not a seamstress!"

"You can't be a faerie, Luella," Ridley said incredulously. "That's impossible."

Luella marched over to the table, stood with a hand on her hip, and proceeded to explain to Ridley how he was most certainly wrong.

Lady Rosalind sighed and stood from the table. "Ridley, you may be excused. Luella, you may sit with your sister. I will be with you in a moment. I want to show you a new stitch today."

Luella did as she was told. Ridley gathered his slate tablet and the rock they used to scratch out letters and placed them on a small shelf near the fireplace.

"Oh, Ridley," Devlin called, "Mr. Danby has a repair needed on his saddle. He would like you to assist him. Is he free, Lady Rosalind?"

"Yes, of course," she replied. "Ridley, let Marta

know that you are to assist Mr. Danby before you go."

Ridley smiled and ran from the room.

Lady Rosalind walked to where he stood. She stood close, and he looked down into her face. Her brown eyes were expressive and intelligent and her skin was flawless. And she smelled good, like roses.

"Thank you for that," she said.

"For what?"

"For being decent and honorable with the children. Other than Benton, no man has ever treated them kindly."

Devlin reflected for a moment and remembered that there were only a few that treated him kindly when he was a young boy too. He remembered the fear and loneliness. He then felt sentiment or possibly jealousy, for these children and their unconventional family arrangement. They'd basically lived in a hell house all their lives under the thumb of Lord Capell, but still, they laughed. They played. They learned and grew.

Devlin's heart jumped slightly in his chest. Was this what Alden often spoke of, having a family, friends and caring?

Stop it!

He was here to do a job, and that was all. Besides, look at him. He was a beast, a cold-hearted killer. He could not comprehend how Rosalind could even look at him.

"Did Lord Capell keep ledgers or records of collected rents and funds? I would like to see an accounting of his transactions. If he owed a debt, that person could have been a threat."

"I believe he did. Just off from his bedchamber is his private library. He often went to that room in the evenings. If he had records, they would be there."

"Good. I will see what, if anything, there is to find. I do not wish to be disturbed," Devlin said curtly. He left the room.

****

Rosalind followed him to the door of the solar and pointed down the hall where Lord Edmond's bedchamber door stood closed. She stared after him.

This man…this man who she knew to be dangerous and held her future in his hands confused her. His questioning was firm and sometimes intimidating. But nothing he had asked was unfair. Stories were told of his ruthlessness on the battlefield. But there was more to him than that.

He tolerated jests and banter from his friend Alden, and her heart fluttered when she saw he was patient with the children. Devlin looked menacing, but when he spoke to the girls and Ridley, his scarred face softened, and his dark eyes showed amusement and interest, not cruelty, like he enjoyed their company—or at the very least didn't despise their presence.

And whether he realized it or not, he gave Benton and Marta quiet respect. He hadn't spoken as if he was better than them. His closeness with the king placed him in a position of power but he treated them with dignity. This behavior conflicted with her initial assessment of him. Maybe she was wrong. Perhaps he was honorable. Perhaps he could help her.

But could she trust him?

Chapter Five

In Capell's private study, Devlin pored over the ledgers. The man was unprincipled and an unbearable drunk, but he kept very thorough records. Rents were collected regularly and noted, but Devlin found no other receipts for anything related to the Capell estate except the occasional sale of horses.

It was obvious Lord Capell had not worked any of his lands for some time. Devlin picked up the thick ledger and tried to slide the heavy tome back into the drawer from which he had found it earlier. But the book did not seem to fit in the space. Devlin pulled it out and reached toward the back of the drawer. His hand slid over a much smaller volume. The book had been hidden under the larger ledger.

He opened the leather cover and saw Edmond's script on the parchment pages. It didn't appear to be a journal, but rather a collection of lists. In the left margin of each page, only a single initial was recorded. Directly across from the initials, different amounts of money were written. Often, the words "debt" or "paid" were included beside the number. Gambling records… Most of the entries were modest amounts. However, three listings piqued his interest. The first two read:

J 50 sovereigns (paid)
B 25 sovereigns (paid)

These entries were recorded two months prior. But

the most recent entry was recorded just before Edmond's disappearance, and the amount astonished him. *K 100 sovereigns (debt)*. Edmond owed someone a very large amount of gold. It was possible that "K" tried to collect this debt, and perhaps the attempt escalated into murder. But Capell had constantly lamented that he had no money, and around the manor, there was no show of wealth. Was this a debt that had accumulated over time? Had Edmond sold off family heirlooms to fund his less-than-honorable proclivities? None of this made sense.

He continued his research, but it didn't take long to view the remaining pages. Devlin found no other entries of interest, so he placed the volume back in the drawer. He looked up at the shuttered windows and light showed through the edges between the stone walls. His stomach growled, and he wondered if he had missed the evening meal as he hadn't heard any sounds within the manor for a while.

He exited the study and paused for a moment to view Lord Edmond's chamber. The room was stark, much like the great hall, and contrasted with the warmth and welcoming atmosphere of the solar that he had visited earlier. Here, the floors were not warmed by any rug. The walls were bare; not a single tapestry or painting was hung. There weren't any personal items in view, and the large bed was covered with only a woolen coverlet and a single pillow cushion. The room certainly didn't seem adequate for a favored earl of King Charles I.

Devlin walked from the room and down the stairs to the hall. The warmth of the fire beckoned him into the room and he hadn't realized how cold he had been working upstairs. No one was present except for Alden, who sat in a chair with his large feet pressed toward the hearth. Grim was at his feet.

"Aw, there you are, friend. Come sit here and warm yourself." Alden gestured to the empty chair beside him. "If you're hungry, Marta left some food on the top of the oven. She said it would most likely stay warm for a bit if you needed some sustenance after your work."

Devlin was indeed quite hungry and was touched by her thoughtfulness. In his experience, if you didn't show up at the table at mealtime, then that was a meal lost.

"I am hungry, Alden. Let me get the food, and I will join you."

A minute later, Devlin sat at the table and enjoyed some mostly warm roasted chicken with potatoes, leeks, and carrots. There was even a heel of bread left for him to round out the meal.

I could get used to this.

A warm meal, a warm fire…a warm woman. He almost snorted out loud at this line of thinking.

No woman would find a landless knight very appealing. After all, where would they sleep? On the cold ground each night?

Devlin pushed those thoughts aside.

"Did you find anything useful in your search?" Alden questioned when Devlin finished eating.

"That I did, friend. This could be our first breakthrough." Devlin walked to the chair near the fire and sat. " "

Alden leaned forward with focused attention.

"Edmond kept careful records of his rents and the

few sharecrop totals. Payments were recorded regularly from his tenant farmers, as well as some sales and trades with the villagers. So, at first, I found nothing unusual. But his study contained another ledger. This one appears to hold lists of gambling debts and possibly money he lent to others to cover bets and gaming. I found three rather large totals. Two amounted to seventy-five sovereigns that were paid to him just this past autumn. And if that weren't curious enough, there is another entry saying he owed one hundred sovereigns. This entry was made just days before he disappeared."

Alden's head tilted slightly to the side, and a low whistle escaped his lips. "That's a lot of gold," he said. "And who does he owe?"

"That's the thing. There are no names in this book. Only single initials beside each entry." Devlin sighed.

"Someone dealing in that much gold would have enemies. Wealth usually leads to greed, and that brings out the evil in men," Alden stated.

Devlin agreed. Along with too much drink, money often turned sensible men foolish. His religious experiences were few but he did remember a verse about the love of money being the root of all evil. If what his family and servants said was true, Lord Edmond illustrated this truth perfectly.

"Yes, this part of the puzzle must be solved. But not tonight," he announced as he stood.

"Tomorrow is soon enough."

"Agreed, but I think I will sit a bit longer here and enjoy the fire." Alden placed his feet back toward the flames. "Goodnight, Dev."

When Grim saw Devlin leave, he followed a few

paces behind. They climbed the stairs and headed down the hall to the bedchambers. After passing the lady's room, Devlin noticed that Grim stopped at the next door. He tapped the door with his mighty paw, and the door opened enough for him to pass through.

Devlin sighed and followed the dog into the room. This was where the girls slept. There was a bed to the left, and Kaylyn and Luella were sound asleep. Grim jumped on the bed without hesitation. He carefully and gingerly squeezed in between the two sisters. Devlin started to reach for the dog's collar to pull him off the bed before he woke the girls up, but instead the young girls rolled toward his killer hound, throwing small arms around the dog, and in a matter of seconds, their deep sleep breathing continued.

And that... was that, Devlin realized.

But then he heard a slight whimper and then a louder cry coming from the adjoining room. Lady Rosalind was in some kind of distress. His heart pounded, and his body tensed. He gave Grim the hand signal to stay where he was. If someone was in the chamber, he wanted the children protected.

He pulled his dagger from its sheath and paced stealthily to the door. How could someone have entered the manor without Alden, himself, and the dog knowing? But he was ready. Whoever this intruder was would soon regret their decision. He slowly looked around the door frame and into the room.

The fire cast just enough light to see into the far corners of the chamber. There wasn't anyone there. Rosalind was having a nightmare, it seemed. She tossed and turned on the bed, moving her head from side to side. She mumbled unintelligibly, and then a few words he understood.

"Mmm...no...no...girls...I won't... no, don't!"

Devlin contemplated waking her up from the dream that held her in such fear but realized that he would scare her to death, sword drawn and standing over her in her chamber late at night. Thankfully, the nightmare that gripped her seemed to fade, and in a moment, she rolled over and slept peacefully. Her night clothes dropped off her shoulder just slightly, and Devlin was ashamed that his gaze lingered longer than it should have. But as he turned away, he noticed something else. A familiar rage built inside him. Below her shoulder, a long red scar traveled down into her gown. He had seen that wound before. That welt was the result of a beating with a riding crop. And he had no doubt who had caused this injury. He suddenly wished he would find Edmond alive so that he could kill him, slowly! The man was a disgrace.

Rosalind then cracked open one eyelid.

He braced himself for a scream. But she only sat up slightly and pulled her bedspread up to her chin.

"Sir Devlin." Her voice was hushed, her eyes widening. "What in all of the heavens are you doing here?"

"A thousand pardons, my lady," he stammered out quickly. "Grim entered the children's room, and I came in to get him." He motioned towards the door. "But he made himself quite comfortable in their bed. I heard you crying out. I thought someone was in your chamber. So I entered. But it seems you were having a bad dream." He bowed his head. "Please forgive my intrusion."

Rosalind's hands covered her face, and she shook

her head from side to side. When she lowered them, her eyes filled with tears that threatened to escape at any second. "I don't remember what the dream was about. The children tell me I cry out often, but I only know that I wake up feeling afraid."

Devlin wondered if the nightmare was a manifestation of some hidden secret or even guilt. He'd known many men that suffered from the night terrors, and these men were usually reliving horrors of their past each night.

He sat on the very edge of the bed, making sure he didn't touch her in any way. "We all have our own demons to fight at one time or another. But you don't have to fight yours alone. I can help you...if you let me," he said as he looked deep into her eyes.

Rosalind stared back. "Sir Devlin." The words came in an almost breathless whisper. "I only want for Lord Edmond to be found and for him to be alive. The future of the children, Marta, Benton, and myself hangs in the balance." Her voice grew stronger. "I have nowhere to go. Marta and Benton might find placement in another home, but would they welcome Ridley? Kaylyn and Luella have no family. What becomes of them if the king sends me to live under the roof of another guardian? Not many would welcome the gentry children of the ward's dead friend. Living with Lord Edmond was terrifying at times. But at least here we are all together!" And with those last words, the tears that had held for so long finally poured down her face.

Devlin wanted to pull this woman into his arms, hold her, and tell her all would be well. But he knew the odds of Rosalind keeping the family of her heart together were not in her favor. If Edmond was dead, and Devlin believed he was, the king would either marry her off quickly or send her to another estate to live under the guardianship of one of his trusted countrymen. If Rosalind had anything to do with Edmond's disappearance or caused him harm in any way, she would be sentenced to jail.

Rosalind then sat up taller in the bed. She wiped her eyes. "I must not let myself fall into a state of panic. I have to find a way to keep us together. I must!"

Devlin stood, and he did not doubt she would do anything to save her family. But she had calmed now, and he didn't want to be found in her quarters late at night alone without a chaperone. He started to leave but paused. "The scar on your shoulder. Did he do that to you?"

Rosalind looked at him, and tears threatened to fall again, but she only turned away from him, pulled up the coverlet, and shut her eyes.

****

When Rosalind finally heard the door gently close, she threw the covers off herself. She got out of bed and paced in front of the fire. She was troubled, and her thoughts raced out of control once more as she imagined every possible outcome over and over in her mind.

If her guardian was never found, and no one was implicated in his disappearance or death, the future for herself and the children was uncertain. Being Lord Capell's only heir, the king might allow her to stay here at the manor. However much this sounded ideal, it would only be a matter of time before a marriage was arranged. Her husband may or may not settle at Capell manor and if he did, he might not accept the children as

67

her family.

The king could marry her off and claim the estate as his, much like her father's ancestral home had. Or the king might allow her new husband to take possession of her childhood home.

She knew in her heart that Lord Edmond wasn't returning. If only she hadn't argued with him so vehemently. His threats pushed her to retaliate with so much anger and vitriol that she didn't even know existed in her heart.

She went to Kaylyn and Luella's room and looked inside.

For them, I'd do anything...

The girls were sound asleep. Both curled around the massive dog that, in such a short period of time, had made himself a part of their rag-tag family. Grim raised his head and looked at her, and she saw the slightest tail wag.

"You'll keep them safe. Won't you, boy?" she whispered to the dog.

Grim rested his large head back onto the bed, but his ears remained up and alert. Rosalind had no doubt about the dog's loyalty and his desire to protect those who cared for him.

She was calmer after watching the girls sleep for a few moments, and she turned back to her room, found her bed, and climbed under the covers. She took a few minutes to pray and hoped that God would show her the way to keep the people she loved safe and together. After she said her amen and closed her eyes, one face kept drifting into her mind's eye.

It was Sir Devlin.

****

Devlin entered his cold bedchamber. Ridley had added logs and banked up the coals hours ago. Only glowing embers remained. Devlin stirred the glowing shards of wood and then he added a few small logs to the fledgling flames and after a few moments roared back to life. His thoughts raced.

He paced the floor in front of the hearth and thought of Lord Edmond. The more he learned of the man, the odds that he was alive were slim. And everyone in this household had the motive to kill him.

But Rosalind was right. The best possible outcome for herself, Marta, Benton, and the children hinged on the old man being alive. At least for a time, they could stay together. He pondered if this valid assumption cleared suspicion from the lady and her loyal servants, because harming Capell would bring too much risk to themselves.

After a few more rounds of pacing in the chamber, he gave up and changed into his nightshirt. He climbed into bed, and when he closed his eyes, her image remained.

Chapter Six

The next morning, Rosalind entered the kitchen and found that Alden and Sir Devlin had already left the manor.

"Only grabbed a hunk of cheese to break their fast!" Marta exclaimed.

"Said they were going to search again for any sign of Lord Capell."

Rosalind's stomach flip-flopped, but she joined the children and Benton at the table. Without the king's men in the manor, Rosalind pretended that everything was back to normal and that today would be a regular day; the children would complete their lessons, chores would be done, and for now, she refused to ponder their precarious future.

She sipped her tea and tried to eat as best she could. But she could only stomach a few bites of dry toasted bread. She laughed inwardly at her paltry attempt to push her worries from her mind, and her thoughts quickly returned to reality. Today would not be typical. She knew she would sit and worry about what the men might find, and she shuddered. She knew her only hope was to stay busy, or her anxious thoughts would render her paralyzed.

As they finished their breakfast, Rosalind and Marta planned the meals for the next two days. Benton and Ridley noted that more wood needed to be hauled in for the kitchen and bed chambers and that the stable needed to be mucked out. Rosalind told the girls they would help with dusting and sweeping several rooms upstairs and down. These additional duties would be done after the beds were made and lessons completed. The girls only grumbled slightly but were agreeable to the day's plan.

****

Sir Devlin and Alden had risen just as the first sliver of gray light was seen upon the eastern horizon. It had been two days, and still, there was no sign of Edmond Capell anywhere. Devlin thought a more organized search of the Capell lands was warranted.

"We'll look around the manor house itself and the work in circles moving outward. I want to be able to tell the king that no part of Edmond's estate was left unchecked."

Alden nodded, and the careful search began.

The morning air was crisp, and a wind from the north bit any exposed flesh as they rode. The sun never made an appearance, and the day remained gray and overcast.

"Alden, I want to talk to the farmer again. The one who found the horse," Devlin said after their two-hour hunt had yielded nothing. "What was his name again?"

"Henry," Alden replied. "He discovered Capell's mount, and his young son returned it to the manor."

They turned the horses southward, and Alden led the way.

When they arrived at Henry's cottage, the man was outside trying to gather his goats and herd them into a rough lean-to shelter. He looked toward the riders as they rode closer and threw up his hand in greeting.

Devlin waited as Henry rounded up the last goat and shut the ramshackle gate behind the animals.

"Good day, sirs," he said pleasantly. "What can I help you with?"

"Good day, Henry," Alden began. "Sir Devlin has been tasked by the king to find Lord Capell. He had a few more questions for you about the horse you found. Capell's horse."

"I'll tell you what I can, but it's not much. You already know what I saw that morning," Alden replied.

"Yes, and the information was most helpful," Alden assured him. "But Sir Devlin seeks a few more details."

"When you found the horse, did it appear that anything was missing from the animal?"

"No, no.. nothing at all," Henry shook his head. "Just as I said before, its fine tack was all there, and even the saddle bag was still attached to the saddle."

Devlin already knew this information, but he pressed on with another question.

"Was there anything, anything at all that was unusual about the horse? Think, Henry," Devlin said seriously.

Henry thought for a moment. "Mud," he finally said.

Devlin's head cocked slightly to the side. "Mud?" he echoed the farmer. "What would be unusual about mud?"

This was England in the winter. Mud was practically everywhere.

"It was the type of mud, sir. This was mud you see in the bog. The horse was covered from the hoof almost to its hock in thick bog mud. My boy and I tried to remove what we could with a quick curry before we took it back to the manor, but the beast looked like a mess."

"And where would the closest bog be, Henry?" Alden inquired.

Henry pointed toward the south. "Just over that ridge. It'd be another ten minutes or so to get there."

Devlin glanced at Alden, and then they both looked toward the sky. Henry was right to be sheltering the livestock. Thick, dark clouds were building; a storm would soon be upon them. Their search would have to wait another day.

The men thanked Henry and left the farmer to his work. Once out of earshot, Devlin turned to his friend.

"Why didn't Benton or Ridley think to tell us about the state of the horse when it was returned? The mud could pinpoint Edmond's last known location."

Alden had no answers, but it was clear now that information was being deliberately withheld.

"Don't mention anything about this to anyone. The storm looks close. We will have to continue our search of the bog tomorrow."

Alden nodded, and as the wind began to pick up in earnest, they turned their horses toward the manor house and concentrated on getting there before the clouds released their cache of snow.

Devlin breathed a sigh of relief when the manor house was in view. By the time they reached the stable, the wind howled, and small particles of ice circulated in the air. Ridley was there, spreading fresh straw at the end of the barn that housed the chickens. Even the ducks had come in from the small shelters erected around the small pond where they spent their days. The birds were more than ready to leave the cold environment outside and come into the barn. Like the fowl, Devlin was appreciative of the shelter. The normally skittish chickens walked directly past him and settled into the confinement of the barn.

The storm's going to be bad.

Alden and Devlin unsaddled the horses, and Ridley, now finished with the chickens and the goats, rushed to help the men. He wiped each horse down with soft cloths while Devlin saw to putting fresh hay in the mangers. Alden grabbed two buckets and filled them with fresh water from the well outside the stable.

"Glad you made it before the storm," Ridley said. "I think it could be bad tonight."

"Agreed," Alden replied. "We've made it back just in time."

"Supper is almost ready," Ridley continued. "Marta was worried that you hadn't eaten all day."

Alden grinned at that. While hungry, Devlin also wanted to kick his feet up in front of the fire. The cold had penetrated his bones. A quiet evening with a warm meal and a hot fire beckoned him.

With the horses and the other livestock comfortable in the barn, the two men and Ridley hurried through the downpour of sleet along the path that led from the manor to the barn.

Devlin opened the door to the manor and was not met with the warmth and calm they desired but with shrieks from Luella. Both men tensed and grabbed their swords.

"No! No! No!" Marta screamed.

From the kitchen, Grim appeared, tail tucked between his back legs. He carried a large ham roast in his mouth, so large he could hardly see where he was going. Kaylyn chased the dog closely, yelling at him to "drop it," which Grim had no intention of doing. Marta was not far behind, and she had a large rolling pin. Devlin was sure she would use it on his hound, and deservedly so. Little Luella chased all three, panicked that Grim was in trouble and would get hurt.

"Enough!" Devlin shouted in a menacing voice.

Everyone, including the dog, stopped.

"Grim! Drop that ham!" The dog instantly obeyed and everyone in the entire room stood frozen waiting for Devlin to speak again.

Devlin took a deep breath and pain shot through his temples. "Marta. Please accept my sincerest apologies. I assume that our supper is on the floor?"

Marta nodded, looking defeated. "I'll see what I can salvage." She gathered the ham in her apron and carried it back to the kitchen.

Devlin turned to Luella, who was still crying loudly. He scooped her up in his strong arms, and held her close. She began to calm almost instantly, but still hiccupped from her panicked crying.

Grim still sat on the floor, but only a smear of ham grease remained in front of him. He had the gall to lick it off the floor and look surprised at all the fuss.

"Please don't hurt Grim, Mr. Devil," Luella squeaked. "He didn't mean it."

"Well, young lady, I will need to disagree with you there. I believe that naughty hound seized that ham with no hesitation and without any thought of our hungry bellies. I can only hope that Marta will forgive him."

Luella giggled and then sniffled.

"Grim!" Devlin barked. "Go lie down!"

The dog obeyed instantly and made his way to his blanket on the rug by the fire.

"Kaylyn, you and Luella see if Marta needs help in the kitchen. Luella, wash your face."

The children trotted off to the kitchen. Devlin hadn't noticed that Rosalind stood at the doorframe. He had no idea how long she had been there. Had she witnessed his ill-mannered dog trying to escape with the dinner ham?

"Please forgive the chaos Grim has caused you, milady. It seems the ham was too much of a temptation for him."

"You won't harm him, will you?" Rosalind asked with a hint of fear in her voice.

"I will certainly punish him if you want. Or at least kick him back out to the stalls."

"No, I don't want him punished. Look at him. I think he's ashamed of his behavior." Rosalind glanced over at the table.

Grim had now moved under the table and looked guilty and regretful. He refused to make eye contact when Devlin leaned over and looked at him.

Devlin snorted. "I don't think it's me he needs to concern himself with. Marta may bring out her skillet again."

Rosalind giggled. Devlin took a step toward Rosalind and started to say something, but then Benton arrived to announce dinner.

"Marta is now ready with this evening's meal, milady and Sir Devlin. She has saved enough ham for us to sup upon tonight, but she has informed me that Grim is not to receive one morsel from the table."

The last comment was directed at Rosalind, who

was known to sneak Grim a few tidbits from her trencher at each meal. Alden, who had been watching his friend and his interactions with the children, the dog, and now Rosalind, grinned.

"Can I join you for dinner?" he asked. "Or maybe you two would prefer to dine alone?" Alden asked with a slight chuckle of his own.

"What? Please sit...yes. Dinner." Rosalind gave her head a slight shake, and turned to Benton. "We are ready now. Please bring out the meal when you are ready."

Rosalind, Alden, and Sir Devlin took their seats, and it wasn't long before Benton, followed by Ridley, carried two trays to the table. The once substantial ham was now whittled down to one-third its size. The portion that had hit the floor when Grim was ordered to drop it had been cut away, and the top side that Grim had in his mouth was removed as well.

However, Marta had performed a culinary miracle, and the table was full of other delicious fare to fill their bellies. Marta had sent out blocks of sharp, yellow cheese, dried fruit from the larder, and the bread she had saved for tomorrow's breakfast. And, of course, there were plenty of potatoes, parsnips, and a turnip or two. The meal was hearty enough, and both men and Rosalind ate their fill. Grim, on the other hand, made no attempt to beg for a tasty tidbit, nor did he stand by the table and wait for a stray crumb to fall.

The storm that threatened Alden and Sir Devlin as they rode toward the bog now raged in earnest. Ridley had come in twice during dinner to throw more wood into the fireplace. But despite his efforts, the great hall remained drafty and cool. The wind thrust its way through every minute crevice in the masonry and found every weakness in the few shutters that were closed and sealed for the winter season.

As Rosalind finished her meal, she asked, "Did you find any information of value on your search today?"

Alden looked toward Sir Devlin and nodded imperceptibly, encouraging Devlin to answer.

"No, unfortunately, we didn't. We widened our search perimeter and talked to everyone we could, and no one told us anything helpful. It's like he disappeared off the face of the Earth that evening. Disappeared without a trace."

Devlin hated lying to Rosalind. But his gut told him that she knew more than she was telling, or others knew more and were protecting her. The horse had come back with bog muck up to its hocks. Ridley and Benton would have known that was where the horse had been, but they failed to tell this to Alden or himself. And Rosalind may or may not have known of this potentially critical piece of the puzzle.

Devlin wanted to change the subject of conversation off of Edmond, but Luella and Kaylyn chose to run into the hall, both dressed in their night clothes.

"Mama!" Kaylyn yelled. "May we stay up a bit later? Please! The wind is howling, and Luella is scared."

"And our room is too cold," Luella added pitifully.

"I added wood to their fires, milady," Ridley offered. "The rooms will warm soon."

"Of course, you can stay with us here a bit," Rosalind said. "Go and get your playthings and sit closer to the hearth."

Rosalind rose and made her way to her chair on the rug, where she joined Grim and the girls. She had a woolen shawl cast over the back of the chair, and she wrapped it around herself. She then sat and picked up her sewing from her basket.

By now, the table had been cleared, and Ridley had returned from the kitchen. He pulled a small table and two stools from the south edge of the room and procured a chess board and pieces from a box that was nestled under the table.

"Mr. Danby, do you care to play?" Ridley asked.

"I would be happy to trounce you at a game of strategy, Mr. Ridley," Alden said confidently. He moved to the small table and set his pieces on the board.

Luella and Kaylyn had dumped a small basket of wood carvings of some sort onto the rug. Each piece was a simply carved animal or person. There were ducks, cows, chickens, people figures, and even a few trees carved into wooden toys for the girls. It wasn't long before the girls had constructed a farm on the rug, with Grim in the middle serving as the "mountain" between the girl's farm and the village that was currently constructed of kindling wood.

Benton and Marta emerged from the kitchen a few moments after, and each took a chair and pulled closer to the fire. Marta had her own sewing basket from which she began embroidering on an apron. Benton acquired a simple box from the mantle. From the box, he took out a block of wood and a carving knife. Devlin wondered who had gifted the girls with such valuable toys, and now he knew. Benton kept a cloth in his lap, and he started carving.

"What are you making there, Benton?" Devlin asked.

"Kaylyn tells me that they need some fine draft horses for their collection," he replied. "A horse is a challenging figure to form with my knife, but I strive to do my best."

Devlin had no doubt he would deliver a couple of perfectly acceptable horses for the girls' play farm.

Devlin leaned back into his own chair and stretched his feet toward the fire. He observed this odd family he had come to investigate.

None were of blood kin, but this small clan had forged bonds as deep and loyal as any family he had ever known. The howls of the wind didn't bother the family as they worked and played near the comforting warmth of the fire.

****

Rosalind glanced up from her stitching. Devlin looked thoughtful. He was relaxed, and she saw the raw handsomeness of his face. His thick black hair curled ever so slightly at his ears and the nape of his neck. He had a prominent brow that, when angry or frustrated, would lower and pull closer together over his thick-lashed, near-black eyes. Yes, she'd seen plenty of his angry looks. But not now. Now his eyes were soft and looked almost kind, a stark contrast with the jagged scar that ran from the corner of his eye to the line of his strong jaw.

His lips, not overly full, smiled and revealed white teeth. He must have heard something amusing while listening to the girl's chatter as they played before him on the rug. Her gaze ventured to his arms and chest. His broad shoulders and chest tapered into a trim waist. His thick, muscled forearms rested on the arms of the chair. Suddenly Rosalind wanted to remove her shawl despite the manor's chill.

"Ridley! You clever lad! I think you've got me!"

Alden's booming voice thankfully interrupted her admiring assessment of Sir Devlin that left her smoldering.

"It will be check-mate in three moves unless you're smart enough to figure out how to get out of it!" Ridley boasted loudly.

Devlin looked surprised that the boy would beat Alden in the game.

"He was taught by the best, Mr. Danby," Rosalind said.

"And who might that be?" Alden asked with a ready smile. "Who is the Capell Manor chess master?

"That would be Benton," Rosalind said with a proud smile. "I've never known him to be defeated in a match."

"Sir Devlin, do you play?" Rosalind asked.

"I can hold my own at the chess table."

Rosalind nodded. "Did your father teach you?"

Devlin's expression turned cloudy. "No. No, my father, though a brilliant strategist, didn't play games. He was much too...serious to ever engage in such pursuits."

"Your father, what was his trade?"

Rosalind noticed Devlin's posture change. No longer looking relaxed, he seemed uncomfortable, and his lower jaw flexed.

"My father was a hired soldier as his father before him. He worked for whoever could pay him the highest price."

Rosalind thought it wise not to seek more information about his father.

"I'm sure he wasn't around much, then. What about your mother? Where did you grow up as a child?"

He snorted. "You're right. He wasn't around much." He took a gulp from his tankard. "My mother died having me. And my father, not being a devoted family man, left me in the care of some distant relatives. They were kind enough, at least from what I can remember." He paused and seemed lost in the past. "But as my father aged, he returned home more often between tasks. He taught me everything I know," he said with a clipped laugh.

Rosalind lowered her head to her sewing and wondered if she should continue to ask about Devlin's past. But suddenly, a loud banging was heard from the foyer. Marta dropped her mending. The children looked up, and Grim leaped from his lounging position on the rug to an immediate alert pose. The dog glanced at Sir Devlin for instruction. Alden and Sir Devlin reached for their swords that were never far from their persons.

"I don't suppose you are expecting anyone, milady?" Devlin asked.

Chapter Seven

Rosalind quickly folded her work and placed it in the basket. She took a step toward the incessant thumping coming from the manor entrance.

Devlin held up a hand to stop her, "Are you expecting someone, milady?"

Rosalind quickly replied, "No. No. Of course not. And who would be out on a night like this?"

"And it's getting so late, too!" Marta added.

Benton rose from his chair, and Ridley sat with Luella and Kaylyn.

"Benton and I will go see who our surprise visitor is. Alden, you stay here."

"Grim! Stay!"

Everyone did as they were told.

Benton and Devlin left the room and turned the corner. Once out of sight, Rosalind's heart beat even faster. Yes, Alden was there, and Grim was too. But she would have felt better if Devlin were there with her and the children. Unannounced, late-night visitors rarely brought good news.

"I'm here to collect what is due to me!"

Rosalind jumped at the booming voice. She turned to Marta, and Marta looked back at her with an expression that was oddly angry and full of fear at the same time.

"Rosalind is coming with me! She's coming with

me! Now!"

And then silence.

Alden stood ready. A tense moment passed, and then another.

Finally, Devlin rounded the corner back into the great hall. He was followed by a man. He stood slightly taller than Devlin but had a slim build. The hood of his cloak covered his head and half of his face. Rosalind knew who it was the moment he bellowed from the foyer. Roland Kirkeby. Bile rose to her throat.

Calm yourself.

From the brief time she'd known Sir Devlin and Alden, she was sure they would not let this man unleash his fury in this household. But she needed tell them why Roland was there. She had hoped Roland would drop his petition, but no. He wanted what he thought was rightfully his.

****

When Devlin entered the dining area the children backed against the hearth, huddled together. And Rosalind looked like she would lose her dinner at any moment. He noticed, too, a slight tremble in her hand as she nervously fingered the collar of her tunic.

"Milady," Devlin began calmly, "This, uh, gentleman claims that you and he are betrothed and that you are to leave with him post haste. Can you explain?"

Before Rosalind could say a word, Roland cut in. "Edmond Capell arranged the betrothal. He said she was mine to take as my wife. He sent the contract to the king for approval."

"I know nothing about any betrothal contract," Rosalind replied with certainty in her voice.

Red anger traveled up Roland's neck and into his

face. "You lie!" he yelled.

However, Grim stepped forward to stand next to his mistress. With ears forward, he crouched low in his haunches, and the fur on his neck rose. A low growl erupted from deep in his throat. Devlin knew this posture well. Grim was ready to pounce. If Roland took one more step toward the lady of the house, his throat would be ripped out.

Alden now stood next to Rosalind and in front of the children, effectively showing his support and protection for them all.

"If you value your life, Kirkeby, I suggest you back away." Devlin was cold but calm.

Roland glanced at the dog, then Alden, and he stepped back slowly. He then turned to Devlin. "Edmond and I had an agreement. Rosalind is to be mine."

Rosalind shook her head, and Roland's rage spilled out again.

"You knew. Yes, you did! I was here the night Edmond told you of the contract. You did know of the betrothal!"

Devlin's stomach sank each time Roland contended that Rosalind was his to marry.

Rosalind's anger now matched Roland's. "You listen to me, Roland Kirkeby. After a night of gaming, when both you and my uncle were so drunk you could barely walk, I was told I was the prize of a card game! Now, if you think that is a binding agreement, I beg to differ! I stand by what I said. Lord Edmond never told me or showed me a contract. Ever!"

"The lady has spoken to her side," Devlin said. "I think you need to leave now. If you believe this contract exists, then you can inquire with the king's clerk."

"How dare you. How dare you speak to me in that manner. You dirty whore! You've lain with these men, haven't you? Bewitched them into believing your lying mouth? You wait, Rosalind Capell, I'll teach you your place." He raised his arm and shook his fist.

Rosalind flinched and stepped back. And that was all it took for Grim. The dog leaped at Roland. In only a second, Roland was pinned, and Grim clasped his throat in his massive jaws. Roland screamed in pure fear. He tried to get out from under the dog, but his efforts were futile.

Devlin noticed immediately that Grim only held Roland. The dog's teeth had not penetrated the soft flesh of his neck. Devlin wondered briefly if he should just give Grim the kill command. This particular problem would disappear in a matter of seconds.

Roland writhed under the dog, and finally, Devlin told Grim to let him up. As much as he'd like to see this odious man gone, Roland had the motive to see Edmond dead. If Capell had promised Rosalind to him and then broke the deal, Roland would have been angry enough to kill him. Devlin needed to investigate further.

Grim returned to his place by Rosalind, and Ridley and the girls moved to stand next to him. Ridley placed his hand on the dog and gave him a pat. Kaylyn told him what a good boy he was. Luella just wrapped her arms around the hound and hugged him tightly. Grim reached around with his massive head and gave Luella's cheek a gentle lick.

Devlin assumed his dog was ruined by all the love and attention, but he realized he was wrong. Grim now had more motivation to protect those to which he was loyal.

Devlin turned to Roland, who somehow pulled himself into an upright position. But, it seemed his legs refused to hold his weight as he had propped himself up against the leg of the table. He breathed heavily.

"I am going to tell you what I expect of you, Roland Kirkeby. Listen well. The day after tomorrow, I will ride to your estate. You have until then to prove to me that a betrothal contract existed. Unless proven, I will assume it never existed."

Roland started to protest.

"Shut it! As is your right, you can send a message to the king's clerk and request verification of your so-called agreement with Lord Capell. Delivery of a message and then a reply will take several days, so let me make this clear. You are not to set foot on the Capell estate until the circumstances of Capell's disappearance are discovered and we know if there is any truth to your assertions. Understood?"

Roland nodded weakly.

"Alden, please assist Roland outside. I'm not sure he can make it on his own."

Alden grabbed his arm, and walked him—dragged him, actually—toward the foyer and the door. When everyone in the room heard the large entrance door open and shut, Rosalind and Benton let out a collective sigh; poor Marta fell back into her chair. No one spoke for a moment, but finally, Rosalind broke the silence.

"Children, it's late. Let's get ready for bed. Ridley, take the girls upstairs," she announced.

Surprisingly, there were no protests or complaints. Normally, the children would have picked up their wooden toys, but not tonight. Ridley grabbed the hand of each girl, and they turned to leave.

"But I want Grim to stay with us," Luella said pitifully as she walked toward the stairs.

Devlin knew there was a catch. Grim, hearing his name, turned to Devlin as if to ask if he could go. With a wave of his hand, Devlin sent him with the children.

When the children rounded the corner, and their steps were no longer heard, Devlin addressed Rosalind. "It is late, milady. But I must know more about Kirkeby and his dealings with Lord Edmond. The evening has been shall we say, eventful, but the matter is urgent."

"Yes, of course. I'll tell you what I know." Rosalind moved back to her chair and sat.

"Did Lord Edmond promise you in marriage to that oaf?" Devlin asked bluntly.

Rosalind inhaled audibly. "Yes, I do believe he did."

Devlin's temper threatened to explode. "Why wasn't I told? Kirkeby could have information about Edmond's disappearance or even have the motive to kill Edmond. I feel like I am running in circles. I need the truth, and I need it now!"

She inhaled again and began her tale in a soft voice. Her voice trembled as she gazed at the floor. "I think you realize by now that Lord Capell was a despot in this household, a sot, and cruel towards the children and myself. But what I am about to tell you brings me so much shame to say. I never truly believed the depravity of my uncle until that night with Roland. I cannot understand how anyone, much less the brother to my dear father, would do what he did." A single tear slid, unchecked, down her face. "Uncle planned a night of gambling and drinking here at the manor. This was not uncommon. He often had men from the village and others that lived closer to the border here for drinking and whoring and who knows what else.

"On the nights when there were men here, the children and I stayed upstairs in the solar and then we all slept together in my room, even Ridley. Marta and Benton stayed downstairs and monitored the stairwell and the great hall to ensure no one wandered around the manor. That night, we heard the usual yelling and swearing. We had fallen asleep, but we were all woken up when Roland stormed into my chamber. He was so drunk he could barely walk, and his speech was slurred. But, he kept saying he won me fair and square, and he was going to take what now belonged to him."

Devlin could hardly sit still in his chair.

Why did I call Grim off? How could I have let that bastard walk out of here?

His head throbbed, and a red-hot rage built in his chest.

"I yelled at Ridley and told him to get the girls and run. I knew if he could get them out, they would go to their hiding place. No one knew where it was, and they would be safe. I threw off the bedcovers and jumped from the bed. That drew Roland's attention solely to me, and Ridley had the girls out the door in seconds." Rosalind stopped. She was still looking down at the floor, and her chest rose and fell. She swallowed hard.

Devlin sat for a moment in silence and then asked in a quiet, calm voice. "What…what did he do then, Rosalind?"

Her gaze flickered and met his. "When the children ran, he looked at me. He looked at me, and he smiled. I thought for a second about the evil in that smile, and I tried to run. But he moved so fast. I couldn't get away. I tried to get out the door to the girls' room, but he hit me hard." Rosalind's hand rose to her cheek, and she caressed her face softly, lost in the memory, and once again looked at the floor.

Devlin's heart threatened to beat out of his chest. His jaw clenched while he waited for her to continue.

"I must have blacked out because when my eyes opened, he was on the bed. He was on top of me, ripping my nightdress from my shoulders. I screamed once, and he slapped my face." Rosalind was visibly shaking now, and she looked up at him then.

"Did he rape you, Rosalind?"

She shook her head furiously. "No, that bastard did not."

Devlin didn't realize he had been holding his breath, and he exhaled.

"Benton came in just in the nick of time, and he yelled at him to get off of me, and he grabbed the poker from the fireplace. It was enough of a diversion, and I was able to get out from under his hold."

"There is no way that Benton could beat him in a fight," Devlin commented. "What happened?"

"True," Rosalind agreed. "But he would have to fight both of us then. I had my dagger, and Benton was so brave. He was ready to fight to the death if needed."

Devlin didn't doubt the old servant's loyalty to his mistress, and likewise, Rosalind would have killed for the old man in a second.

"But it never came to a fight. Uncle Edmond rushed in. He grabbed Kirkeby and told him he couldn't have me...yet. The king would have to approve the contract, and he wouldn't allow Roland to "ruin me" for future suitors if the king refused the union."

"Oh, wasn't that considerate of him?" Devlin said sarcastically.

She was quiet for a moment. "I was only a bartering chip to my uncle, a way to increase his wealth. He didn't even comment on my swollen face or ripped clothes."

"That I am not surprised about. But what about the contract, milady? Did your uncle send the request to the king?"

"Of that, I am not sure. After he and Roland left my chambers, I could not sleep. Marta sat with me, and finally, at dawn, I drifted off to sleep. I awoke around noon, and Uncle Edmond was still asleep. The drinking from the night before must have hit him hard. But when he finally awoke, he did not speak of what happened the night before or the contract. Truthfully, I was afraid to ask. And secretly, I hoped that in a drunken stupor, he had promised me to Kirkeby, but in the light of day, he realized the folly of this contract and didn't go through with it."

"But Roland didn't forget, did he?" Devlin said, almost to himself.

"No. No, evidently not," Rosalind replied.

One small droplet escaped from her eye and cascaded down her cheek.

He reached out and caught the drop before it reached the bottom of her face. His touch was gentle. He then gently lifted her chin, and his whisper-quiet voice was chilling as he said, "Roland Kirkeby will never have you."

Chapter Eight

The hour was late, but Devlin knew he would not sleep. He ordered Rosalind upstairs to bed. She seemed to have the strength to walk, but just barely. He watched her as she turned the corner, and he stayed in the great hall until he could no longer hear her footsteps on the stairs.

And then he paced. The tension built inside his body until he feared he would explode with the force of it. Alden had not returned to the manor house since he had escorted that lout Kirkeby out, so Devlin headed out to the stable himself. He secretly wished that Roland was still on the premises. He could immediately handle this problem, and no one would ever know.

He rounded the corner into the barn. Alden perched on a crude bench against a stall door, and surprisingly, Ridley was there too. Ridley held his head in his hands, and despite the dim light from the single lantern hanging from an iron hook on the post, Devlin could see that Ridley was crying.

Poor kid. The events of the evening had certainly taken a toll on the young lad.

"Devlin, come sit."

Alden's tone indicated that there was more than met the eye. Devlin wondered what else could happen that night that would top what had already transpired.

"Sir Devlin," Ridley began, "You need to know

what I did."

Devlin said nothing. It took a moment before Ridley could speak.

"There was a marriage contract," Ridley stated. His face paled considerably. "I took the contract from Lord Edmond. He told me to take it to Ned in the village, and Ned would see to it that it was delivered to the king. But I couldn't, Sir Devlin. I told Lord Edmond I had completed the task, but I took the contract and hid it. I couldn't let him give Lady Rosalind to that scoundrel."

Devlin was speechless. He reeled with the news and was glad he was sitting.

What the boy had done was incomprehensible to him. To disobey his lord, to interfere with kingdom business in this way would result in a severe flogging in the least and possibly even death if anyone ever found out.

Devlin grabbed Ridley by his skinny shoulders. "Ridley, listen to my questions and answer them truthfully."

Ridley, with eyes open wide, nodded with sincerity.

"Did Ned know that Edmond was sending him a missive to deliver to court? Did he know of the betrothal promise between Edmond and Kirkeby?"

"I don't believe he did. He wasn't here when Roland won milady in the card game. And the old lord didn't speak with him any time after that."

Devlin exhaled audibly in relief.

"Do you have the message that Lord Edmond penned to the king? Do you still have the contract?"

"Yes, I do. It's hidden where no one will ever find it."

Devlin nodded. "And did anyone else in the household know of the contract or know that Edmond sent you to deliver a message to Ned for the king?"

Ridley thought for a moment. "No one else knew. Not Benton, not Marta, and milady didn't know either. And I didn't tell anyone."

He had to consider all the possible ramifications of this bit of information for Ridley and Rosalind. If no one else knew of Edmond's intention to send the contract to the king that day, and if Edmond was dead, there would be no consequences. Roland knew, of course, but it would be his word against Rosalind's, and with no contract, he could not prove anything. And Devlin was willing to take the chance that the king would not believe that Roland "won" her in a card game as payment for a gaming debt.

But if Edmond were alive, the consequences would be dire for Ridley, and Rosalind would most likely be married off to Roland as soon as he was found or returned.

"Ridley, you keep that message hidden, do you hear? Don't tell anyone where it is. Not even me. Do you understand?"

Ridley nodded vigorously again.

"Now, I must talk with Alden. You get back to your bed. It's too late for you to be up and about."

Ridley turned to leave. But very quickly, he ran to each man, and hugged them both. After the quick gesture of thanks and affection, he hurried from the stable toward the manor house.

"I guess he thought you would punish him on the spot. Or worse, threaten to turn him in," Alden said.

"Punish him? No. What he did was wrong and very

dangerous. Surely, he couldn't understand what would happen to him if his deceit was found out. He obviously loves her very much."

"We already knew that Ridley had a hatred for Capell, and his love and devotion to Rosalind is unquestionable," Alden added. "And now we know how far he would go to keep her out of the clutches of Kirkeby and further out of any harm's way. Do you think the boy could have had a hand in Edmond's disappearance?"

Devlin nodded and considered the possibility. "All the evidence points to the bog. We know that Edmond, well at least his mount, was there. As far as we know, Edmond was, too. Weather permitting, we will return there in the morning. We'll search again."

The men gave the barn a final once over, checking to see that the horses were secure. Alden picked up the lantern, and they walked to the manor house in silence.

****

Devlin was awakened before dawn with the now familiar sounds of Ridley adding wood to his fire. Never in his life had anyone ever worried about his comfort. No one had ever cared whether he had woken up in a warm room on a cold morning before. But here, in the midst of so much pain and hostility, this clan cared for each other and wanted to care for others as well. Devlin didn't know what to do with this unfamiliar feeling.

But no matter. Today, he and Alden would venture out once more. There had to be something there. He threw back the covers and pushed himself out of his warm nest. He doused his face with water that was left in a pitcher by the fire. She thought of everything. No cold water for washing in this house; the water was kept warm for his use.

As he left his bedchamber, he closed his door; Alden exited his room at the same time. His face, normally pleasant and smiling, was downcast. It appeared that neither man was looking forward to another trip to the bog.

Down in the great hall, Benton had just laid out the morning's breakfast. Devlin wasn't hungry, but he knew he should eat. He grabbed a bowl with porridge, some fresh bread, and a wedge of cheese. Alden joined him at the table, but they ate in silence.

Rosalind and the children were not seen before they left. But that was understandable. The night before had been quite stressful, and no one retired until late. Alden grabbed some bread and cheese to take with him. At the stables, Ridley had each of their mounts saddled and ready. Dim light filtered through the thick clouds, but the sun didn't make an appearance. The morning was damp and cold, but at least the winds died, and the snow and sleet stopped.

The men mounted their horses, and after only a few steps, Alden asked, "Do you really think Edmond is in the bog, Devlin?"

"All I know is that the only clue, the only real evidence we have leads there."

"But why was he out here, in the middle of the night, no less? Think about it. He's over an hour's ride from his home, town is in the opposite direction, and none of his drinking or gaming cohorts live in this direction. There are only a few farmers' and crofters' cottages about."

Devlin had not thought about Edmond's motives.

Alden asked good questions. Why was he this far out, late at night? It truly made no sense. But Devlin knew he had to find out. As they entered the area containing the low-lying land, the forest landscape began to change. Fewer trees grew, and the dark, rich soil of the forest floor, once solid beneath the horses' hooves, softened and turned gray.

They had arrived.

Devlin surveyed the uneven border of the mire. They certainly had their work cut out for them.

"Let's search in opposite directions around the wettest edge of the bog. Look for any sign of Edmond or the horse."

Alden nodded, turned to his left, and methodically looked around the edges of the bog. Devlin began his own search, working in the opposite direction of his friend.

The cold quiet of the marsh was interrupted by the occasional caw of a crow in the distance, and it wasn't long before the men met back where they had started and had nothing to show for their hunt.

"What now?"

Devlin let out a deep sigh, "Now I go in."

Alden shook his head, but he understood that it had to be done. Devlin removed his cloak and he took a moment until he found a sturdy branch that matched his height.

Devlin moved side to side across the watery bog, and when he could no longer see the bottom under the murky water, he used his stick to poke down to the depths. The water was icy cold, and when the first tiny hints of the frigid liquid leaked over the top of his boots and down his calves, he clenched his jaw. But he refused to give up.

At first, the bog didn't seem deep enough to conceal the body of a man, but as he moved to the center, its depth increased. Devlin continued to step and poke, step and poke. Every so often, his boot would stick in the mud, and he would have to reach into the filthy pool and use his hands to free his foot. Alden stood by, ready to assist if necessary.

And then, when he was ready to give up, his stick hit something. He moved the stick and poked and prodded. "Alden! Toss me the rope from my saddle," he commanded.

Alden threw him the length of rope, and he fashioned a quick loop.

"Devlin, are you sure?" Alden asked.

Devlin nodded, and then he did what he had been dreading most. He took two deep breaths and dove under the water. He kept his eyes closed and relied on his hands to explore what he had found. It didn't take long before he knew.

It was a body.

With the rope around the body's legs knotted securely, he rose from the mire.

"It's a corpse, Alden. It's got to be Edmond."

He spat water and shook his wet hair. He climbed from the muck slowly. When he got to the dry bank, he grabbed a blanket from his saddle bag and wiped his face. He was freezing, his teeth chattering, but he wanted to see…he had to see.

With the rope tied to his saddle, he slowly backed his horse away from the bog. The rope stretched taunt, but slowly, the bog released its grisly prize from its depths. Once on shore, Devlin and Alden got their first look.

It was Edmond. His face had decomposed somewhat, but due to the mud and the cold weather, Devlin could make out his features, and further, his cloak bore the family crest. Devlin dropped to his knees. His shaking and chills hindered his movements, so Alden grabbed his friend from behind.

"Devlin, man, you must get out of your wet clothes."

Devlin nodded. "Don't touch him. Wait for me."

Devlin quickly changed into trousers and a shirt he had packed with him and he grabbed his warm cloak. He then returned to the body.

There was no outward evidence of any injury that he could see. He looked up and down the water-logged form. He bent down and carefully examined Edmond's legs and arms and felt no breaks, and there were no rips or tears in his clothing. Devlin was ready to call his death an unfortunate accident. Perhaps for reasons unknown, Edmond's horse was spooked into the bog, or maybe it was too dark; Edmond rode his horse too close to the edge, and he and the animal got stuck. Devlin was elated. He could tell the king it was an accident.

He peeled back the edges of Edmond's cloak and sought out the inner pockets of the garment. Inside, he found a small dagger in the left upper side pocket. When he reached into the larger pocket, he found a small leather pouch. Upon opening the pouch, he discovered twenty pieces of gold and a few silver pieces as well. Devlin wondered about the money, but he was glad he found it as this would support his theory that Edmond was not robbed and this whole thing was an unfortunate accident. Devlin rolled him over.

There were bulges and lumps in the back of his trousers and large ones at that. Upon closer inspection, he discovered heavy rocks had been crammed into his pants, and large flat stones wedged into his waistcoat and belt.

Devlin sighed loudly. His accident theory now had an unfortunate snag. Lord Edmond's body had been weighed down. Whoever did this hoped he'd never be found.

Alden shook his head, "Dammit! But who would take the time to sink his body and not take the gold? It makes no sense!"

Devlin shrugged and sighed. The brief hope of there not being foul play was gone.

"Let's get him wrapped up, and back to the manor." Alden went to his horse to get the extra blanket he carried with him.

Devlin noticed something in Edmond's shriveled hand. It was a chain with a locket. He picked the necklace from the dead man's grasp, and opened the locket. The locket contained two miniature pictures painted inside. It was a man and a woman, and he didn't know who they were. But his gaze fixed upon the miniature portrait of the woman in the locket, and he began to see a resemblance with the long, curly dark hair and the eyes. He quickly stashed the jewelry in his pocket before Alden returned to his side.

The men wrapped the body in the two blankets they had and then draped Edmond over Alden's horse. The ride home was slow and solemn, and Devlin pondered what direction his investigation would go now.

"I am going to suggest something. And I want you

to think about it before you answer. Devlin, you are the most loyal man I know. And you never break a promise or a deal. That's why the king trusts you with his more, shall we say, delicate matters. But in this case, I can't see any good reason why we can't just say this was a terrible tragedy but also just an accident. No one will ever know that the scoundrel was weighed down in the bog. We don't have to mention that we found signs of foul play. We can report back to the king and be done with this."

Devlin was quiet for a moment. "I want nothing more than to clear Rosalind and her servants. No, not servants. They are her family. None of them deserve to face any punishment or consequences of any kind from that bastard Edmond and his cruelty. But we have too many loose ends. Kirkeby, for one. He thinks the betrothal contract was sent to the king. When he finds out it never made it, he will never believe that Edmond died in an accident. He will try to implicate Rosalind, or at the very least her family, to help his case."

"We could kill him," Alden said matter-of-factly.

"You don't think I haven't thought of that?" Devlin replied quickly. "I have enjoyed the possibility of ending Roland Kirkeby in a variety of different ways since he made his appearance and intentions known, but I don't think it would help."

"And the king," Devlin continued. "I don't think he will believe an accident, in a bog, in the middle of the forest when his man had no reason to be out here. And let's just say he did believe our story. Rosalind and the children are sure to be separated. The king will marry her off, and who knows what will happen to Ridley, Kaylyn, and Luella. They are the children of servants and not titled in any way."

"Sounds like Rosalind needs an acceptable suitor then. Someone who is ready to settle down and who will accept the children…and the unconventional servants. Someone who is loyal to the king and who will watch his border closely. Hmm, I wonder who could… and would fill this unique position," Alden said with a grin, and a sparkle in his eye.

Devlin stared at Alden, and after a stunned moment of silence, he said, "Are you mad? You don't think I should marry Rosalind? I'm…I'm not…I'm not what she needs. She is a titled, gentle lady. I have nothing. I can give her nothing. She'd probably run in the opposite direction, screaming at the thought."

"I think you underestimate the lady of the manor, Devlin. She's strong and brave. But more than that, she isn't interested in jewels, fancy gowns, or gold. She wants her family together and to be safe, Devlin. You can give her that."

Devlin shook his head. He saw no way that the king would grant him Rosalind's hand. A marriage would give the king a measure of security, sure, but he wouldn't gain any lands marrying her off to his hired man.

Chapter Nine

When Alden and Devlin rode their horses to the stable, no one was around, and he was glad. The noon hour had long passed, and he assumed everyone was busy in the house with chores, lessons, and such.

Devlin took Lord Edmond down from the back of Alden's horse, and he placed him inside the barn at the back of the hall. The weather was still cool, and so the body would keep for a time. Devlin had the smell of the bog on him. He wanted more than anything to take a bath. But he knew he had to let the household know what he'd found. He headed toward the door to the kitchens, and every step up the path seemed heavier and more challenging to make as he got closer.

He and Alden entered the kitchen, and Marta took one look at him, and she knew. She gasped, and her hand flew to cover her mouth.

Devlin nodded. "Where is your lady?"

Marta cleared her throat and answered, her voice quivering, "She's in the solar, Sir Devlin. With the children."

Devlin left the kitchen, climbed the back stairs to the second floor, and entered the chamber that Rosalind used as a school room. The children were seated around the table. Ridley worked on his sums, and the girls both wrote on their boards. Rosalind monitored their work. Grim appeared to be passed out, enjoying his rest in a square of sun that streamed through the glass window. When Devlin stepped forward, the dog raised his big head, snorted in Devlin's direction, and then returned to his nap.

That dog has become way too comfortable.

Then he turned to Rosalind, and she caught his expression. He didn't have to say anything.

"You found him then?"

She was not surprised, and her face was emotionless. Devlin didn't know what he'd expected, but no emotion was a surprise.

"Ridley, continue with the girls and help them with their letters and reading. I'll be right back."

Rosalind closed the door behind her as they left the room. By now, Benton and Marta, escorted by Alden, had joined Devlin in the hall. Rosalind quickly opened the door to Edmond's bedchamber, and immediately closed it so they could talk without the children hearing.

"Tell me," she said right away. "What did you find?"

"Edmond. He was at the bottom of the bog."

Devlin searched everyone's face. Marta looked genuinely surprised, and then she clenched her jaw. upset, Her hands shook ever so slightly. Benton looked stoic as he always did. His face gave away nothing. And Rosalind now looked nervous and curious.

"Could you tell if he was injured?"

"Did he have his sword?"

"Was he robbed?"

Devlin told them. He looked at everyone in the room and tried to discern from their faces if this news was surprising and unknown to them. Marta looked pale, horrified, actually. Rosalind was also pale but not necessarily shaken. And Benton appeared unaffected by the news that his lord had been rotting at the bottom of a bog.

"Then it was an accident then. We don't know how he landed in the bog, but it seems that he must have got stuck in the mire and drowned," said Benton.

Suddenly, Rosalind gasped and yelled, "Marta!"

Benton moved in slow motion to catch poor Marta as she swooned into a faint, but there was no way he would catch her in time. Luckily, Devlin leapt into action and caught her before she hit the hard floor. Rosalind rushed to put a pillow under her head, and as soon as she was sure Marta, while prone and passed out, was comfortable, she started to say something.

"I'm not finished," Devlin stated quietly. "I would like to believe that this is true. But I did find something on the body."

Rosalind lifted her gaze to his.

"Inside his cloak was a bag of gold and silver pieces. And that's not all. His body was weighed down with rocks. Large stones were crammed in his trouser legs and his waistcoat. Someone didn't want him found."

All heads turned as Marta began to moan. "I killed him. It was me. It was the nightshade."

Rosalind gasped at Marta's groggy confession. Benton's mouth dropped open.

Alden muttered, "Holy Mother…"

Devlin bent down and helped Marta to sit. "Choose your words carefully. Marta," he cautioned. "Are you saying you poisoned Lord Edmond?"

Marta shook her head. "No, no. Well, yes, I guess I did, But not intentionally. Although he did deserve it, and I wanted to many times."

Devlin looked at the woman as if she was ready to be committed to Bedlam.

What is she rambling about? Was that a confession or not?

"Take a deep breath, Marta," Rosalind said calmly. "When you're ready, tell us what happened."

Marta extended her hand up, and Alden helped her to stand, but her legs remained unsteady. He helped her to a chair by the wardrobe.

"That night—the night that Edmond and Lady Rosalind argued so terribly, I knew that trouble was coming. His mood was nastier than ever before, I tell you. Once Lady Rosalind had run to her chambers, Lord Edmond remained at the table. He had practically passed out not long after she left. And that's how I wanted him. Immobile."

"So you poisoned him?" Devlin asked, not sure where she was going with her recounting of her part in this tale.

"No, no. I only meant to give him a sleeping draft that would keep him out until morning. When I saw he had passed out, I started to clear the table. But after a moment, he stirred a bit and started rambling and cursing about Lady Rosalind again. I ran back to the kitchen to get my tonics. When he sat up, I poured him some water and told him I added a tincture that would help with the headache in the morning."

Under scrutiny, she burst into tears.

"The next morning, when I returned to the kitchen, I realized that I had not given Lord Edmond a sleeping draft. I picked up the wrong jar in my haste! I had given him the nightshade!" Her last words ended in a wail.

Devlin could not believe his ears. Now, another member of this family he had grown so attached to was complicit in the murder of Lord Edmond.

I need a strong drink.

"So let me get this straight. You thought to give Lord Edmond something that would help him sleep so he wouldn't harm Lady Rosalind, and you poisoned him. By mistake?"

"Well, of course, it was by mistake, Sir Devlin. Our Marta wouldn't kill anyone. Not on purpose. She's not a murderer. Shame on you for doubting her sincerity. Can't you see how distraught she is?" Rosalind said.

Marta began to wail again at his questioning.

"I'm not saying she did it on purpose. I can believe her. But I don't know if the king will."

Marta yelled out, "It's over! I'm done for. They'll take my head or lock me up in the tower for sure!" Her wails grew louder, and she looked ready to faint once more.

"There, there Marta. They will not do any such thing. Say, you did give him the nightshade. It wasn't enough to kill him. And you certainly didn't weigh his body down in the bog. There is another person, I believe, who is responsible." Rosalind stated with conviction.

"She's right. Marta certainly couldn't have weighed a body down and hauled it into the bog. We still have too many loose ends here." Alden said.

"All right," Devlin said firmly. "Marta, pull yourself together. I need you to be able to think. All of you, think! Was there anyone who came to the manor or any meeting that Lord Edmond had in the weeks leading up to his disappearance that seemed off? Or a message he received, or any change in his mood that seemed unusual that would indicate something was wrong or that he was being threatened?"

Everyone in the room was quiet.

"Alden!" Devlin barked and made Marta and Rosalind jump. "Get Ridley in here. He knows when anyone comes and goes, and the good Lord knows he moves about without being seen or heard. He may have seen or heard something the others didn't know about."

Alden opened the door to cross the hall to the solar, and Ridley tumbled into the room.

Devlin, not at all surprised, asked, "Ridley, was there anyone unusual in the manor or did you notice any strange behavior out of Lord Edmond in the weeks before his disappearance. This is important, son. Any detail, even if you're not sure it means anything, might help us figure out what happened."

Devlin almost didn't notice that he had called Ridley "son." Use of this term of endearment and the realization about how fond he had grown of the boy shocked and left him bewildered. He had vowed never to have children. After all, what did he have to offer? But no, he felt protective and even more determined to solve this mystery and clear all of them of any suspicion or wrongdoing.

Ridley sat on the edge of Edmond's bed and thought. By now, Rosalind was pacing, trying her hardest to recall any minute detail. Marta sat in the chair, wringing her hands. Her face was white as a sheet and a light sheen of sweat glistened across her brow. Alden had taken a kerchief and fanned her vigorously. Bentley sat in the desk chair and fell asleep. When he let out a very healthy snore, Devlin sighed and gave a defeated shrug of resignation.

But Ridley suddenly sat up tall on the edge of the bed. "I may have something!"

"Well, go on then, Ridley, tell us."

Ridley recounted what he had seen and heard just a few days prior to Edmond's disappearance.

"I was doing my morning work like I always do. The sun wasn't up yet, and everyone except Marta was still asleep. I took some firewood to the lord's bedchamber. I was super quiet because I didn't want to wake him. I put the firewood in the wood holder there. I stoked the fire and added a log."

"Ridley, get to it," Devlin prompted. "We know you stoke fires each morning already."

"I was about to leave the room when Lord Edmond started thrashing and moaning in his sleep. He had done that before, especially after a night of drinking and whorin'."

Rosalind gasped, and Marta sat straight up in her chair. "Ridley Shaw! You watch your tongue. And around our lady too! I'm not so far gone over here that I can't get up and box those ears!"

Both Devlin and Alden hid a grin. Neither doubted that Marta, nearly in a dead faint or not, wouldn't follow through with her threat.

Ridley quickly apologized and continued his tale. "At first, the sounds he made were just his usual miserable moans and groans. But then he started talking, almost yelling, really, as he thrashed about. Some of the words were hard to make out, but he kept saying two words over and over."

Everyone leaned in, waiting for Ridley to reveal

Edmond's sleep talking. Ridley paused dramatically.

"He said freedom whispers."

Devlin started pacing, Marta fell back into her chair, Alden commenced fanning her again, and Benton, who managed to wake up for Ridley's disclosure, snorted in exasperation.

Devlin turned to Rosalind. "Does that mean anything to you? Have you heard it anywhere before?"

Rosalind shook her head.

"Are you sure that is what he said?" Devlin asked.

"Oh yes. I am sure. He said it over and over and even yelled it out a couple of times."

"Was there anything else, Ridley? Anything else that seemed amiss the day before or around that same time?"

"Yes, there was," he said. "It was his desk."

"What about his desk, Ridley?" Rosalind asked. "I was here in the days before and the day after Lord Edmond disappeared and nothing looked amiss."

"That same morning, I noticed that the desk was askew in the room like it had been pushed away from its place on the floor, and most of the drawers were open. There were papers scattered about and even some on the floor. And the inkwell…it had tipped over, and there was ink everywhere."

"Did you look at any of the papers, Ridley?" Alden asked eagerly.

"No! Definitely not. If the old lord had woken up and caught me snooping around the desk, I'd have got a thrashing for sure."

"Marta, did you clean up the papers or ink?" Rosalind asked.

"No, milady. I never saw anything like that, and I

always tidied the lord's room every day after the morning victuals."

"Benton, what about you? When you helped your lord dress that morning, and really every morning, did you see anything unusual?"

"Not a thing, milady. The room looked much as it does now. Nothing looked out of place."

Rosalind thought for a second. "It does seem Lord Edmond was upset about something. But then again, he was often in a rage. It could have been anything."

"So basically, we're no closer to figuring this out since we found the bloke." Alden sighed.

"Not entirely true, Alden," Devlin said. "We have the words he kept repeating in his sleep. It could be a clue."

Marta, who had finally composed herself, stood and announced, "Nothing is ever solved easily on empty stomachs. We'll sup early this evening." And with that she left the room.

Chapter Ten

Rosalind gave Devlin and Alden a nod and then called to Ridley, "Come Ridley, we've left the girls to their own devices way too long. Let's finish our lessons."

Devlin followed Rosalind out of Lord Edmond's room, and Alden was close behind.

"We'll be down shortly," Rosalind informed them. Then she entered the solar and quietly shut the door behind her.

Alden and Devlin descended the stairs. Both men sighed as they sat in chairs in front of the fireplace.

"It's got to mean something. What Ridley heard from Edmond; don't you think?" Alden said after several quiet minutes.

"Does it, you think? Those words. They could have meant nothing…just ramblings from a drunk old man."

"I don't know. The way the papers and ledgers were tossed about the room and the fact that the he cleaned all that up before Benton arrived that morning to see to his lord's dressing is very suspicious. The cryptic words—I think it's all related. Something going on, something to hide. Why else would someone have weighed the ol' bugger down in the bog?"

Devlin stared into the flames. What Alden alleged had merit. But what was he missing?

Ridley bounded down the stairs and ran through

the great room and into the kitchen, interrupting his thoughts. A few minutes later, Benton followed. And then it wasn't long before Rosalind, Luella, and Kaylyn joined them by the fire.

Rosalind sat in her rocking chair and grabbed her mending basket. Sensing the seriousness of the mood, the girls didn't grab their toys, but rather Kaylyn picked up a sampler she'd been working on and practiced her stitches, and little Luella started rolling the newly spun yarn skeins into balls that were resting beside Marta's basket. No one seemed in the mood to talk.

Ridley returned with a tray laden with mugs of ale for the men, hot tea for Rosalind, and cups of hot cider for the girls. Rosalind smiled softly and took several sips of her tea. The girls enjoyed their cider treat, and it wasn't long before Luella chatted happily with herself about a new adventure she'd made up in her imaginative mind.

"What do you think, Mama Rose?" Kaylyn asked as she held up her sampler.

Rosalind looked carefully at the stitches Kaylyn had been meticulously applying to the fabric. She smiled and replied, "These are perfect, Kaylyn. All your hard work and practice has paid off."

Kaylyn beamed at the praise she received.

"Sups ready!" Ridley boomed as he carried a tray to the buffet from the kitchen.

"Ridley Shaw!" Marta yelled from the kitchen. Then the round woman pushed the door open. "Mind your manners! Since when have you announced dinner in such a fashion?"

Benton followed Ridley to the buffet, carrying a soup tureen and ladle. The old man shook his head slowly from side to side, but he didn't admonish the boy.

"Sir Devlin, milady, Mr. Danby, girls, please come to the table."

Everyone took their seats. Ridley passed out the bowls, and Benton moved carefully to ladle soup in each one. Then Ridley placed two round loaves of rich rye bread between the diners.

****

Rosalind watched as the men eagerly soaked chunks of bread in their soup and ate enthusiastically and she wondered if there was anything that squelched a man's appetite. It wasn't pulling up a rotting body from the bottom of a bog, obviously.

"Do you think we'll have some more snow?" Luella asked, with eyes wide.

The child was eager to try out the sled that Benton had crafted for her. The last storm proved to produce more ice and rain and her results sliding down the hill behind the manor proved quite unsatisfying.

"It's possible, Luella. It is certainly cold enough."

"Did I ever tell you about the time I slid down a hill straight into the jaws of a hungry bear?" Alden piped up.

Kaylyn and Luella stopped eating mid-bite, and their mouths froze open.

Rosalind smiled, "Oh, please do tell us about this adventure, Mr. Danby."

"Alden," Devlin interrupted. "I don't believe that ever happened. As I remember it, you slid down a very steep hill on your sled straight into a huge pile of horse shi…I mean horse dung outside the livery stable where you were supposed to be working."

Alden's grin turned mischievous, "What do you think, girls? Do you want to hear the story, as I know it happened?"

"Oh yes, please!" Kaylyn said. "But wait, I must get Ridley!" And she bounded out of the room, with Luella following after.

"Your story will be a welcome distraction from this trying day, Mr. Danby. I'm sure we'll all enjoy it. But while the children are gone from the room. I have to ask. What do we do with Lord Edmond? I mean for a funeral or burial."

"Do the girls know he's dead? Did you tell them?" Devlin asked, his voice low.

"Yes. I told them when I went back to finish their lessons. They were not upset in the least."

"I wouldn't think they would be. But there will certainly need to be a ceremony of some sort."

Devlin nodded in agreement. "I want to take a closer look at his body. I want my report to the king to be thorough, and I need to be sure I'm not missing anything. The king won't accept anything less. When I'm done, we can plan Lord Edmond's burial."

Rosalind heard the children come through the hall that led to the kitchen. They were arguing on whether the upcoming tale from Alden was true or not.

"There's no way he sleds into the jaws of a bear, Kaylyn," Ridley argued. "He'd be dead."

"Perhaps he wrestled the bear? And won!" Kaylyn shot back. "It could happen, you know."

Luella, not to be left out, said, "I bet it was actually just a small bear. Men tend to exaggerate, you know."

Rosalind stifled a giggle. "Go to the fire and get settled. Mr. Danby will tell you his account of this harrowing story when he has finished his meal."

A moment later, Benton entered the dining area with another tray. This one was laden with hunks of yellow-orange cheese, cold beef left over from the day before, and some dried fruit. Marta followed after him with more warm cider.

"I hear there's a brave tale to be told here," she said as she placed the tray on the table.

"That there is," Alden replied. "You are welcome to join us, and Benton too. But I can't guarantee you'll sleep a wink tonight after hearing it!"

Devlin rolled his eyes, and Rosalind started to laugh, but the loud iron door knocker was heard—a harbinger of nothing good. Silence fell like a heavy, stifling shroud over everyone in the room. The last unannounced evening visitor proved to be quite disruptive.

Rosalind's heart quickened, and she drew in a breath. But just as the panic welled up in her chest, she looked at Devlin. His gaze bore into hers with an expression that told her that he would not let any harm come to her or the children.

Grim rose from his favorite spot on the rug and stood at alert in front of the children and Benton started toward the door, with Devlin walking patiently behind him. The pounding on the door increased. Rosalind's heart beat with each pound and her anxiety rose with each boom.

And then, there was silence. Rosalind looked at Marta and then Alden. Alden shrugged his shoulders. The dog stood at alert, and his ears were forward.

After a moment, Devlin returned. With him was Roland Kirkeby and a young boy. Rosalind was both appalled and confused.

Benton finally caught back up with Devlin and announced, "Milady, young James is here from the village with a message for Sir Devlin. And I'm not really certain of Roland's business here at the manor."

"I'll tell you why I'm here, old man. Shut your trap! Know your place, you ancient relic."

Devlin strode over to Roland and boxed his ears—hard.

"It seems Kirkeby here didn't learn his lesson from his last visit here, Alden. I think he needs another. But first, I need to hear from this lad here. What is your message?"

The boy, no more than nine or ten years of age, wrung his hat in his hands, but he took a step forward. "My message is for Devlin Alastor. The king is sending his man here for a full report on your findings. Edward Kelley should arrive in three days if the weather holds for travel."

Devlin nodded to the young boy. He then turned to Roland, "And why are you here? You were told never to come back."

"I was there when the message from the king arrived in town. I only sought to accompany James on his errand. His father thought it too late to journey out this way, but I assured him I would keep him safe. The matter is urgent, is it not? And I wanted Rosalind to understand that I would be seeking an audience with Kelley when he arrives. I sent my own inquiry to the king concerning our marriage contract. Perhaps Kelley knows the king's decision."

Roland craned his neck and looked around Devlin. He glared at Rosalind. "You won't be able to hide behind these two clods much longer, my dear."

From where she sat, she saw Devlin's jaw clench. She knew the signs all too well when a man turned dangerous. Devlin was ready to pounce. The children needed to be removed from the room immediately.

"Marta, could you serve James and the children some oatcakes with honey in the kitchen?" Rosalind suggested quietly.

"Yes, milady. Children, James, come with me. We'll have a warm treat."

All four children followed Marta, and once the room was clear, Devlin wasted no time. He had Roland by the neck and pinned against the wall in seconds. Roland struggled to breathe as his face turned red, then purple. His feet wiggled as he gasped and tried to break free from Devlin's grip.

"Alden! You can't let Devlin kill him!" Rosalind exclaimed.

But when she turned to see why Alden hadn't made a move to stop his friend, she saw that he had grabbed a mug of ale, sat back in his chair with his feet propped up, and was watching the entertainment Devlin was providing with obvious satisfaction.

"I see no reason to let him live. Do you?" he asked Rosalind.

Rosalind ran to Devlin's side. "Stop! You can't kill him! Think about it! He's sent a message to the king. How will it look if you kill the man who claims to have a marriage contract with me?"

Devlin didn't seem to hear her. If anything, his grip tightened. Roland looked as though he would pass out, and only a shallow wheeze was heard when he tried to breathe.

Rosalind took a chance. She reached out gingerly and placed her hand on his arm. The hard muscles flexed in his arm. If Devlin became angry with her for interfering…

No! He's not like Edmond. He won't hurt me!

"Please think about how his death would look. The king trusts you to be impartial. Killing this pathetic excuse for a man won't help me, and it might shroud your investigation in doubt. Please stop."

Devlin turned his head toward Rosalind. His grip remained tight, but he asked her gently, "Are you sure this is what you want? I can kill him. If you want me to, I can snap his neck, and he'll never be a threat to you again."

As distasteful as Roland was, she didn't want him dead so she nodded. With that confirmation, Devlin dropped Roland to the floor. He immediately rolled over, coughed, and gagged as he breathed.

Devlin crouched beside the man and whispered in his ear, "My lady just saved your miserable life. Never forget that! You're only alive because of her, but make no mistake, I will not heed her request a second time. Do you understand?"

Roland nodded and tried to slip across the floor out of Devlin's reach, but before he could get too far, Alden grabbed him by the arm and dragged him out of the manor. Devlin followed.

When Devlin and Alden returned to the great hall, Rosalind and Benton were the only ones in the room.

He placed his hands on her upper arms and said in a husky voice, "He is not worth your distress or your worry. I won't have it." And he gave her a gentle shake. "I should have killed him."

Once again, Rosalind possessed a feeling of safety that she'd never felt in the presence of men. Other than her father, Rosalind's experiences with the masculine sex were less than ideal and often abusive. But with Devlin, she knew he'd always keep her from harm. And she promised herself she'd pray about it later, but she knew without a doubt that he would have killed for her, and that her heart skipped a beat. Feelings of fear and shock when Roland was nearly killed right in the great hall were mixed with feelings of excitement and power!

She took a breath to steady her voice. "I'm glad you didn't. I think it's better that he stays alive…for now."

Devlin dropped his hands from her arms but she wanted him to pull her close and tell her everything would be all right. But she didn't know that, and he wouldn't lie to her.

Benton had informed Marta that it was safe to leave the kitchen. She and the children, all happy, sticky, and warm, sat before the fire.

Rosalind had almost forgotten about poor James. The child knew he was only to deliver a message, but instead, Roland hauled him out to the countryside in the dark, and then he almost witnessed Roland's demise. But the child looked no worse for wear. He obviously enjoyed his adventure and sweet cakes with Marta, and currently, he was giving Grim excellent scratches around his ears.

"James, I'm sure your father is expecting you back. Devlin, do you think Alden can deliver him back to town? He's the innkeeper, right, James?"

"Yes, milady," James replied.

Alden nodded and left to saddle his horse, and

Devlin and Rosalind joined the children near the fire.

"When will we hear about the bear, Mama Rose?" Luella asked.

"I'm sure Mr. Danby will be happy to tell his story tomorrow. The hour has grown too late for scary tales about bears."

A loud voice boomed from the door to the foyer. "Yes, tomorrow, sweet child! I will regale you with a tale so frightening that you'll never venture into the woods again!"

Luella giggled, and Kaylyn yelled from her place on the rug, "You better, Mr. Danby!"

Rosalind was happy to see smiles on their faces. "All right, children. James must return home and you must head to your beds. Hop to it. Let's go."

The girls didn't go without protest. Kaylyn stomped upstairs but Luella stood her ground with her arms crossed. Devlin looked down at the stubborn child and raised an eyebrow at her defiance. She glared back but then raised her tiny arms up to him. Devlin scooped her up and marched up the steps, following Kaylyn to the girl's bedchamber.

"And you too, Ridley. It's been a trying day. Marta, you see that Ridley gets to his bed. No sneaking out to the stables."

Marta assured her that Ridley would do as she asked, and she turned to the stairs. When Rosalind reached the girl's room, her heart melted, and her eyes welled up with tears. Kaylyn was already tucked into bed with Grim and the dog waited for his second "pup" to join them. Luella stood in front of Devlin and he'd just dropped her gown over her shoulders and was guiding one arm through one of the holes. He looked out of sorts trying to dress one very wiggly four-year-old, but he got the job done.

Once in her gown, Luella climbed into bed with her sister and crawled under the covers. Grim squeezed between each child. Rosalind knew he'd move to the rug in front of the fire once the girls were asleep, but for now, he'd stay by their sides.

Devlin told each girl goodnight and he'd see them in the morning. "Oh, I hope you don't mind. We got up here and the girls just started getting ready for bed and Luella had her gown on backwards and so…"

"You did a fine job getting them to bed, Sir Devlin. I would have had to threaten extra chores at least five times by now before I got them dressed."

Devlin smiled almost shyly, then he looked at her closely. "You need rest too. You have shadows under your eyes."

Rosalind pulled the covers up and kissed each child on her forehead. She walked over to the mirror on the wall, and said agreeably, "I do look ghastly. No, you won't have any arguments from me about bedtime."

Devlin followed Rosalind to the door of her chamber. She stopped and looked at Devlin, unsure how she could put what she needed to say into words.

"You continue to surprise me, Sir Devlin."

Devlin cocked his head to the side slightly, "For what, my lady?"

"In the short time that you have been here, you have made my children feel safe. Maybe for the first time ever. And for the first time in a long time, they see that men, even fierce warriors, can be good. It gives me hope, for even if I cannot keep them as my own for much longer, I know that they have seen that there are men who are strong and honorable. Men who fight for what's right."

Devlin lowered his head and said gruffly, "I don't deserve your kind words, Lady Rosalind, for I fear I am not the man you think I am. I have done terrible things."

"I choose not to believe that. I won't. If you have done terrible things then it was because you had to, by order. And for that, you cannot hold yourself accountable." She paused to catch her breath. "I trust what I see... and what I feel, and the man before me now is honorable. And whatever happens in the future, I know that you will act from a position of truth and justice. This I know, Devlin."

She took his head in her hands and lifted until she could see into his dark eyes. Rosalind placed a soft, chaste kiss on his full lips. "Good night, Sir Devlin," she whispered.

Then she entered her room and closed the door behind her.

Chapter Eleven

Devlin returned to the great hall and sat in his chair by the fire.

What just happened?

He could hardly believe it—she kissed him. That single moment left his thoughts jumbled, but it wasn't just the kiss that unsettled him. She believed him to be a good man. He had never considered himself good. Loyal, perhaps, but good? No. Even as his mind churned with heavy matters—the fate of Lord Edmond, the mystery of who had hidden his body, Rosalind's uncertain future, and the children's safety—he found himself returning, again and again, to the softness of her lips, the warmth of that kiss, and how his heart still pounded deep in his chest.

When Alden returned. Devlin didn't greet him or even acknowledge his presence. Alden stared into the flames and had just started to doze when Devlin finally spoke. "She kissed me."

His friend sat up in his chair, his feet dropped back to the floor, and he looked at his friend. "What? What do you mean she kissed you?"

"She said I surprised her, and she thought I was honorable and just. I disagreed, of course, but she insisted. And then she kissed me."

Alden let out a hearty laugh, leaned over, and slapped his friend across his back. "Finally. A woman who doesn't run away screaming when she sees you!"

"How could she, Alden? She doesn't know me. She's heard of things I've done, and what people know or hear about doesn't begin to scratch the surface of my deeds."

"So what does she say when you remind her of who you are?"

Devlin sighed, "She says she doesn't believe all the rumors. She says if I did do what people say, then it was because I had to, not because I wanted to."

Alden looked thoughtful. "She is mostly right."

"What do you mean, 'mostly' right?"

"I mean, my friend that she is right when she says you've done what you had to do. You had orders. But I think you can agree that you love to fight. You want to battle an opponent, and you want to win—there is a part of you that is bloodthirsty—a part of you that enjoys the fight and sometimes the kill."

Devlin did not disagree, and that scared him. "She would do well to stay away from me, then," he said sadly. "And the children."

Alden's head tilted slightly and in a low voice he said, "Oh, the opposite, my friend. The lone wolf doesn't fare well forever. No matter how fierce, the wolf needs a mate and a pack. He won't last long on his own. Lady Rosalind needs you. She needs someone who'll fight for her. She needs someone who'll protect her children at all costs. That person just may be you, Devlin."

"That's the biggest load of horse dung I've ever heard, brother!" Devlin cried out. "Since when do you go all poetic and soft? She doesn't need me! She needs a titled gentleman, one who is generous enough to take in the children. One who can fill her wardrobe with fine clothes and can ensure she never scrubs a floor or slaves in a kitchen again. How could I ever give her any of that?"

Alden looked his friend squarely in the eye. "Would you...if you could? Would you marry her and raise the children as your own? Would you take her and the children in if you had the means?"

"Yes. Yes, I would, and Benton and Marta too, if they would come with us."

Alden nodded. "Then we'll find a way, friend."

"But what if she is a murderer, Alden? What then?"

"Do you think if she did do such a thing, it would have been under the direst of circumstances? I can only see our sweet lady committing a crime if it was to protect herself or her family here."

Alden stated the obvious, and Devlin fired back, "Of course! She doesn't have a greedy or evil bone in her body and would never get enjoyment from someone's demise. You know that. And I know that. But the king? Would he even care? His moods are like the wind. He could be merciful one minute and then cruel the next. Can't you see how he might make an example out of anyone who threatens those who are loyal to him? I fear I won't be able to save her, Alden, no matter what. If she is guilty, or even just the most likely culprit, then the king will do as he pleases, and I'll be powerless to stop him."

"Then we must prove she is innocent," Alden stated matter-of-factly. "Let's start now. I know there has to be more to Ridley's account than what he described. I'm going back up to Capell's study, and I'm going to keep looking."

"I'm coming with you."

The men climbed the main staircase and passed the lady's chamber and the girls' room. Alden peeked into the room. The fire still burned brightly, and the girls were snug under the covers. Grim slept at the very end of the bed. The dog raised its massive head and tilted it to the side, as if to ask Alden what he needed and how dare he interrupt his sleep.

Alden came back into the hall and just shook his head, "That dog has turned into the children's nanny."

Devlin didn't argue. When they reached the lord's chamber, the cold air from the unused room hit them squarely in the face. Devlin felt the chill in his bones. He lit several lanterns, and the men went to work on Capell's desk.

Devlin started by moving the ledgers he'd pored over and placing them on a small side table across the room. Alden sat in the desk's chair and took every object and paper from each drawer, and Devlin examined them. Once each item was scrutinized, Devlin took them to the side table. The desk didn't have much in it overall, so it didn't take long to empty it completely.

"Well, that's it," Alden announced reluctantly.

But Devlin wasn't convinced. "There's got to be something."

He traced each edge and corner of the desk with his hand. There was nothing out of the ordinary. He then took out each drawer, turned them over, and peered inside the drawer space. Nothing there either. He even crawled under the desk and examined the underside, but again there was nothing.

Devlin sighed in frustration and anger burned from his core as he wanted to hit something. He paced the length of the room, and a few expletives escaped his mouth. He was at a complete dead end, and Kelley would be here any day now.

"Wait just a minute," Alden said quietly.

Devlin rushed back to his side. "What have you found?"

"The front panel of the desk—part of it is recessed," Alden said as he showed Devlin where he found the abnormality in the workmanship.

Alden pulled on the small section of wood, but nothing happened. But then he ran his finger underneath and discovered a small lever of sorts. He slid the lever over, and a hidden drawer popped open just slightly. The compartment was only slightly bigger than Alden's hand.

"Well, what do you know?" Devlin smiled as he reached inside and found a thin, leather-bound book. He opened it to discover it was another ledger with numbers and dates recorded.

Just like the larger books he'd pored over before, the writing existed of only one or two initials and an amount. However, there was a notable difference here. All the entries listed were paid to Lord Edmond. There were no notes of money that he owed anyone recorded.

Devlin smiled and looked at Alden, "I think we have a real motive here, friend. It appears that several people were paying Lord Edmond regularly, and whatever it was for, he kept it hidden."

"I agree. There's no telling what that man was delving into. He was a disgrace. Still, our case would be stronger if we knew who was paying him and why."

Devlin nodded and turned a few more pages in the small book. At the end of the book, the last three pages showed several dates and times recorded. Each one was written, then crossed out. Except for one, which had a location scribbled beside it as well.

Wisbech, The Boar's Head, January 18, Dusk

"January 18. That is tomorrow," Alden said.

"Then Wisbech is where I will go," Devlin stated firmly.

"Finally, a real lead. I think we'll find that Capell was up to no good. Let's just hope there will be enough evidence that shows someone would want him dead."

"We can hope, friend, we can hope."

The hour had grown very late. Alden announced he would retire to his bedchamber, and Devlin did not argue. And even though his body was heavy with the strain of the day's events, his spirit was light. As he dropped into his bed, his mind reeled over all the questions he needed answered to solve this puzzle and save Rosalind, the children, and the quirky servants he had grown so fond of.

****

What is that wretched noise?

Devlin had no idea what time it was. Ridley had not tended his fire and dawn's light wasn't seen through the cracks in his window shutter. Devlin let loose a few choice expletives, a loud sigh, and leaped from his bed. He threw only his breeches on and stomped out of his room.

Someone was pounding on the manor door incessantly, he realized at the top of the stairs. Alden emerged from his room, dressed only in his drawers, which weren't cinched at the waist. Sword in one hand

and the other holding up his knickers, If Alden engaged in a fight, it just might evolve into a battle likened to Viking berserkers, when in a bloodthirsty rage, rid themselves of their clothing and fought naked.

"Who in the bloody he—" Alden started to rant but stopped when Rosalind opened her chamber door, her wrap tied around her.

Devlin took in her tousled hair and sleepy eyes and thought she never looked more beautiful. She glanced at the two scantily clad men but wasn't surprised in the slightest.

"Lady, do you know who is responsible for this wretched knocking at this early hour?" Alden asked politely.

Rosalind simply shook her head and shrugged her shoulders.

The men and Rosalind quickly trod down the stairs to the entry hall. Devlin marched to the door and swung it open. Minute snowflakes floating in the frigid predawn air blew into the entry of the manor house. Before him stood a man, short of stature and clothed in fine robes.

Devlin knew who this was. Not from his face but from the two guards that flanked his side. Each carried the king's banner. The coat of arms consisted of three lions and a shield divided into four quarters. The fleur-de-lis of France was in the first and fourth quarters, the lions of Scotland in the second, and the harp of Ireland in the third. He'd carried this banner into many conflicts.

****

Lady Rosalind blushed in embarrassment. She could only imagine what was going through the clerk's mind. There were two half-naked men at her open door, and she stood there only in her night dress and wrap. Oh, the impropriety! But still, there wasn't anything she could do now.

"Mr., uh, Mr. Kelley, I presume. Please, come in."

Devlin and Alden stood in the doorway and refused to let the man and guard pass through for a second or two. Rosalind could tell that Devlin was wary of this man. She placed her hand discreetly on his muscled shoulder, gave him a little pinch, and he finally moved to the side. Edward Kelley grunted as if he was extremely inconvenienced by being there and entering. His large eyes bulged from his head, and he looked down his pointy nose with disdain at his surroundings.

"The fire is warm in the great hall, Mr. Kelley. Please go take a seat and warm yourself."

By now, Ridley was awake, and he stoked the fire in the grand fireplace feverishly to ward off the cold in the room. Benton, slightly disheveled because he'd dressed so quickly, had arrived and directed the royal entourage into the hall.

"Woman!" Kelley barked at Rosalind, "Warm ale! Now!"

Devlin moved faster than a bolt of lightning, grabbed Edward Kelley by his fine cloak and raised him nearly off the ground. His guards immediately took offense and drew their swords. Alden, in turn, stood at his friend's side, grasping his sword with both hands. His knickers fell to the ground and puddled at his feet. Marta entered the great hall, took in the entire scene with a shocked gasp, and dropped the tray of hot drinks she carried.

"I will show you only a bit of grace here, Mr.

Kelley. We've shown ourselves in your presence, let's just say, not in our best light, and you obviously do not know who you address. But that "woman" is the lady of the house, Lord Edmond Capell's niece, Lady Rosalind, and will be afforded the respect that is due to her. Am I clear?"

Edward Kelley was speechless, but he managed to nod his head, and quickly called his men to stand down.

"Alden, retrieve your pants," Devlin said. "I think Mr. Kelley will mind his manners more closely now."

Without taking his eyes off the guards, Alden made himself more decent and backed away from his friend.

"Oh, goodness," Rosalind said with a slight smile as she turned to Ridley, who stood with his mouth wide open in surprise. "Quickly, bring more drinks out to our guests and then we'll help Marta clean up that mess."

To Edward Kelley, she said politely, "It was an easy mistake, Mr. Kelley. We certainly didn't expect you until the day after tomorrow, and you caught all of us still abed. We were quite surprised to hear the pounding on the door. Sir Devlin tends to be a bit prickly when he first wakes up. And Mr. Danby, well... well, him, I'm not too sure about, especially now. Please excuse me while I make myself more presentable. Benton will see your needs whilst I dress."

Rosalind retreated up the main stairwell, only to race down the back servant's steps again to the kitchen to help Marta. She hadn't quite recovered. Rosalind found her sitting in a chair with a cold compress on her forehead.

"Really, Marta! Everything is fine. Our guests from the palace are warm and comfortable and sitting by the fire. With some hot drinks, they'll be fine. Devlin will calm down, and everything will be just fine."

Ridley bounded into the kitchen, poured more warmed ale, and then blurted, "I think Sir Devlin will punch that toad man right in the face. He's just sitting there glaring at him. He's not even making a move to get dressed." Ridley grabbed the tray and headed back out.

"It doesn't sound fine, my lady," Marta replied weakly.

"But it will be." She sat next to Marta, grabbed the compress, placed it on her own forehead, and whispered, "It has to be."

Chapter Twelve

Rosalind sat for only a few moments, then she flew up the back stairs, rushed to her chamber and dressed as fast as she could. She put on the best dress she had. She grabbed a clean linen chemise and over that she placed a tunic. Plain tunics were all she had. This one, however, was dyed a yellow-gold and therefore better suited for being in the presence of the king's representative. It wasn't much, she knew, but it would have to do.

She brushed her long brown hair and carefully fashioned a long braid that fell down her back. As much as she tried to contain her locks, several curly tendrils escaped at her temples and in front of her ears. Now dressed and her hair done, she took a deep breath and decided to look in on the girls and Grim.

They were gone! Rosalind said a quick prayer as she ran down the hall and back down the stairs to the kitchen.

Please, please, let them be in the kitchen!

But they weren't. That could only mean that Kaylyn, Luella, and Devlin's beast were with the king's men. She flew out of the kitchen and rounded the corner to the great hall and took in the scene.

Luella sat in Devlin's lap, wiping a tear from her eye. Except that she wasn't. Rosalind knew that look and it was a ruse usually meant to get attention. Kaylyn sat in Rosalind's chair by the fire and glared at Edward Kelley. Grim stood only a hand's width away from the odious little man; his yellow eyes staring right into his face. His lips were peeled back, and each long incisor dripped with drool. Rosalind heard his low growl from across the room.

"Sir Devlin, I apologize for the children's interruption. I'll get them to the kitchen now." She motioned for the girls to come with her, then she addressed the men. "Marta has the morning meal ready and it will be served momentarily. Thank you for your patience."

Devlin gave Grim the command to heel. The large dog licked his lips and then took his place on the rug close to the fire.

Once in the kitchen, she fired questions at the girls, "What happened in there? Why was Grim going to eat the king's man? And Luella, why were you acting like you were crying?"

"I didn't do anything, Mama Rose," Luella explained. "That man was extremely rude. He said I was bothersome and I didn't know my place. I was just asking him questions, and he tried to shoo me away. That's when Grim jumped up in his face."

"Oh dear," Rosalind fretted. "Girls, listen and listen carefully. You are to stay away from this man, do you hear? I don't know anything about him or his character. He'll report back to the king about Lord Edmond, and we must respect his station. We don't want to make him angry, and the king must think highly of him. Do you understand?"

Both girls nodded solemnly.

"So he said you were a bother, did he?"

"He did. But then I cried a little, and that got Grim upset, and I knew that Grim wouldn't let him hurt me. Oh, and Sir Devlin didn't like it either."

"No, he wouldn't, dear. He wouldn't allow that man to hurt any of us," Rosalind said confidently. "Now, I don't want you to think about Mr. Kelley anymore. Marta has your breakfast here, and I'm going to eat with the grouchy man. After you two eat, help Marta with the dishes and ready the noon meal. If I'm not free when you are finished, go to the solar and work on your stitches. I will be up as soon as I can."

The girls nodded and sat at the table. Benton and Ridley had come and retrieved the serving trays, and she followed them out to the dining hall. Marta had completely recovered from the shock of seeing Alden, naked, ready to skewer the king's men and had outdone herself. With no planning, she had prepared a meal that was fit for the entourage dispatched from the palace.

There were poached eggs, freshly baked bread, two types of jam, sliced roast from the previous evening's meal, dried apples, and porridge sweetened with honey. Benton served each guest and then Rosalind. Sir Devlin had gone to dress, finally, but re-entered the room as his lady engaged the king's men in light conversation.

"I'm sure you are fatigued after your overnight travel, so I had Ridley prepare your room. I'm sure it will be warm and comfortable for you."

Rosalind had not instructed Ridley to do anything of the sort, but she saw him dart from the corner of the room when she spoke.

"As much as I'd like to enjoy a bit of respite here in your humble home, I am here to get a report from Sir Devlin. I will hear about your uncle's disappearance from him as soon as possible. I have no desire to stay here any longer than I need to, so I'll not be wasting any time." Edward Kelley spoke as he looked down his nose at Rosalind.

Devlin entered the room, and before he could sit, Edward declared in his nasal voice that Rosalind suspected resulted from traveling in the cold all night, "Sir Devlin, I will hear your report on Lord Edmond's disappearance post haste. I will speak to you and only you in private as soon as you break your fast. I pray you have news that will satisfy our king. And because I have not seen him yet, I assume he is either still missing or dead, so I'm desperately eager to hear the results of your investigation." The clerk then turned to Rosalind. "Lady Rosalind, do you mind leaving us? If you are finished with your meal, of course."

Rosalind was not fooled by his civil tone. He only did so because Devlin had come to the table. This man wasn't pleased about the task he was ordered to complete, and he obviously felt she was beneath him. But she wouldn't let him rile her.

"Of course, Mr. Kelley. You and Sir Devlin have the room." She stood, relieved and ready to exit, and gave each man a polite nod as she took her leave.

****

Once Rosalind rounded the corner to the kitchen, Kelley turned to Devlin and addressed him without preamble. "I don't need to remind you that the king is feeling quite insecure at this time. The threat from Cromwell and the Parliamentarians grows with each passing day as their popularity grows. Edmond provided King Charles with valuable information, and he now questions the loyalty of many of those he once considered staunch allies. So tell me, man, where is Sir Edmond?"

Devlin took a deep breath. "In short, Sir Edmond lies in the barn. He is dead, and he has been for quite some time."

Edward Kelley sat in silence for a moment. "Continue."

"Upon our arrival, we were shocked to find that only six people live here at the manor. Lady Rosalind, a cook, Edmond's manservant, and three children."

"The children, are they Edmond's bastards or Lady Rosalind's?"

Devlin explained that the children were neither but were the children of servants who had passed away years prior.

Accepting Devlin's explanation about the children, he inquired about Edmond's men. "I, too, find it odd that Edmond's guards are absent. Where did they go?"

"They left when Edmond could no longer pay them," Devlin said flatly.

"From what I see here, Edmond didn't spend his money on the upkeep of his home. It is practically bare of any comforts, and what is here is worn and tired. And the lady of the house dresses practically in rags. I know the king compensated him for the information he provided, and he had funds from Lady Rosalind's estate. Why weren't his guards paid? Where did the money go?"

Devlin was relieved that Kelly had noticed the state of disrepair the manor was in. And he was grateful that he noticed that Rosalind had not been afforded the luxuries of a lady of her title. "He had a weakness for strong drink and spent too much time at the gaming tables. But I think I need to dig deeper to find the true reason his accounts were depleted. I think there was more going on than just losing at the tables."

"And your reason for thinking this way?"

"On the first day after our arrival, I asked Lady Rosalind if Lord Edmond kept ledgers or records. She directed me to his study, and there I found what I expected to find. Lord Edmond carefully considered the rents he collected from the estate lands, the sale of some livestock, and a few other receipts. But then I also found another ledger that recorded debts he owed and those who owed him."

"And do you know who he owed? Any of these men could have sought out Capell."

"No, unfortunately, the ledgers had no names. Just a single initial is recorded next to a total."

"And what of the debts? Were any of enough amount to justify the risk of killing one of the king's loyal and trusted barons."

"In my opinion, no," Devlin stated with regret.

How easy it would have been if that were the case.

Edward Kelley stayed quiet for some time. And when he finally did reply, he posed a question that Devlin dreaded.

"And what of this Roland Kirkeby? His message to the king was quite, shall I say, passionate in his petition. He claims that Lord Capell owed him, and he didn't get his payment due to some interference. What do you know of this?"

Devlin took another deep breath. He'd hoped that Kelley hadn't spoken to Kirkeby or at least wasn't aware of Roland's claim to Lady Rosalind. He knew he had to tell the truth about Roland's claim, but he wasn't going to implicate Ridley in any way. Only Ridley and Capell knew that the contract proposal was drafted, and Ridley was the only one who knew that the document wasn't actually sent. And as far as he was concerned, Kelley didn't need to know about the boy's involvement.

"Kirkeby contends that he won Lady Rosalind in a card game."

Kelley blurted out loudly, "Capell handed his niece over after a card game? That's preposterous! The king would never approve of this union. Kirkeby isn't even titled!"

Devlin was grateful for Kelley's indignation. The man was arrogant, but he seemed to have something of a moral compass. His arrogance could play in Devlin's favor in this particular aspect of the investigation, so he continued with more details.

"Kirkeby claims that he beat Capell soundly, and his winnings totaled more than Capell could pay. Supposedly, Capell offered an all-or-nothing hand. Roland accepted, and he won. When Capell couldn't pay his debt, he offered Lady Rosalind as payment, but he stipulated that he couldn't just take her and that Roland would have to marry her."

"At least there was that," Kelley said dryly. "Still, it is unacceptable, and it never should have been considered. However, Kirkeby claims that Capell submitted a betrothal contract to the king. Is this true?"

"I found no draft of a document in his study nor anything written in his ledgers that would indicate Lady Rosalind would be used to cancel out a debt."

At least that wasn't a lie.

"And Lady Rosalind, did she know what her uncle

had done?"

Devlin chose his words carefully, "Lady Rosalind was aware, yes. I questioned her extensively about the agreement between Capell and Kirkeby. She knew very little of the details except that they were both nearly passed out drunk when the men agreed to this outlandish plan. She was surprised that Kirkeby even remembered. She also added that she assumed the king would never allow it."

"So, she is not fond of Kirkeby then?"

"I think not. He appears to be cut of the same cloth as the uncle. A lover of too much drink and gaming. No, she does not favor him in the slightest."

"It seems to me the person who benefits the most from Lord Capell's death is right here under this roof. It's Lady Rosalind."

Devlin muttered a curse under his breath. He had tried to steer Kelley toward Capell's debtors as the most likely suspects, but he failed. "It is true. If I were the lady, I wouldn't want to be sold off to a drunkard like Roland Kirkeby, but Lady Rosalind? She is too kind. I cannot believe she is capable of murder."

"You'd be surprised at what the supposed "weaker sex" is capable of, Sir Devlin. Look at what she inherits with Capell gone. She is the sole heir to this estate and her father's as well."

"I, too, have considered this. And you are correct. But she only inherits what the king allows. And she knows this. She also knows the king can marry her off to whomever he chooses, and the estates pass to the husband. So, nothing is guaranteed for her. Her place as lady of the manor is not ironclad," Devlin argued back.

"And you are correct in this, Sir Devlin," he

admitted. "But with all she loves and cares about here, I can only think she would want to keep herself and the children safe, at whatever cost. She has much to lose. So, I think it is beneficial to speak with Roland Kirkeby. He might provide more valuable information."

Devlin knew that Kelley would want to speak with Kirkeby, but he had hoped it wouldn't be necessary.

"Now tell me where you found the body of Lord Capell, and did you gain any insight from what was left of the man. Was there evidence left on or near the body?"

Devlin explained how the bog mud found on Edmond's horse led them to the location of Edmond's body.

"Was the horse stripped of the saddle?"

"No, not at all. In fact, all assumed there had been an accident at first because the saddle, bridle, and saddlebag were not stolen. The tenant farmer who found the horse searched for Capell. When his son returned the animal to the manor, Lady Rosalind, Benton, and Ridley went searching as well. They found nothing."

"Danby and I did our own search, too, on the day after our arrival and found nothing. And so that led us back to the bog. Lady Rosalind said the road leading through the bog was a shorter route to Wisbech, but it wasn't often traveled, especially during the wet season. The actual bog was the only place we hadn't searched. It had been frozen solid, but the weather had warmed enough, so I waded out in the mire. About six feet in, I found Edmond's body. Alden and I drug him out."

"And did you find anything unusual?"

"That I did," Devlin stated without emotion. "His

coin was not stolen."

"Well, there you have it. It had to be an accident, then! Why didn't you say so in the first place? Now I can leave this drafty pile of rocks," Kelley proclaimed, and he stood to leave the room.

"That's not all," Devlin continued.

Kelley let out an exasperated sigh and sat back in his chair.

"His pockets and cloak were filled with heavy rocks. He was weighed down. Someone didn't want him found."

The little man shook his head and muttered something that Devlin supposed was cursing. He'd begun to believe that Kelley wanted this mystery solved as much as he did.

He looked up at Devlin, "Anything else?"

"Yes, there is. When we informed Lady Rosalind and the rest of the household that we'd found Edmond, we questioned everyone again and this time we asked if anyone had seen or heard anything unusual in the weeks leading up to his disappearance. Ridley reported something odd."

"Go on."

"A few weeks before Edmond disappeared, Ridley entered his chamber before dawn to stoke the fire as he usually does. He reported that his desk was in disarray, and papers were strewn everywhere. Edmond was calling out in his sleep as well. He kept saying 'Freedom whispers' over and over." He paused and the king's man pondered this new information in his mind. "Does that phrase mean anything to you?"

"No. I've never heard that before," he replied, concerned. "Anything else?"

"And before Benton could tend to Capell that same morning, he'd cleaned up the papers and the room was back as it should have been."

"Did you search for more evidence?"

"We most certainly did, Mr. Kelley. Alden had a sense that we'd missed something, so we searched the desk again and this time we found a hidden compartment."

Kelley was now on the edge of his seat, "Tell me you found something that sheds some light here. I am growing impatient."

"In the hidden space was another journal."

Edward Kelley rolled his eyes, but Devlin kept talking.

"This one was much like the others, a list of initials along with amounts. But all the entries were payments made to Lord Edmond. And, there was one major difference. There was a date and a location written in the back of the journal."

"Go on, man. What was the time and place you saw noted?"

"The note read, "Wisbech, The Boar's Head, today's date, and the time was recorded as 'dusk.' I want to point out that Wisbech is a town not far from here, and the quickest route when traveling there is through the bog. The same bog where Edmond's body was found. Danby and I will travel there today and find what, if anything, can be discovered that could clear up this bloody mess."

"Good. And in the meantime, I will pay a visit to Roland Kirkeby."

Devlin had hoped that Kelley would postpone his visit to Kirkeby so that he could be present during his questioning about the marriage contract, but it was not his place to tell the king's clerk what to do and when to do it. He had to appear completely impartial so as not to cast doubt on Lady Rosalind's innocence.

"But I am quite fatigued, so I'll have a short lie-down before I ride out. Call the manservant to show me to my room." Kelley rose from his chair and paused. "No, that will take too long. Call the boy. I want to get there before tomorrow."

Devlin chuckled to himself. Then he called for Ridley.

****

Rosalind passed the day in a state of anxiety. Edward Kelley had left after the noonday meal for an immediate audience with Roland Kirkeby. Her stomach rolled each time she thought of that wretched man. And each time she allowed herself to think of actually marrying that scoundrel; she thought she'd be physically ill. Surely, Mr. Kelley would see his claims of a marriage to pay off a debt and an actual betrothal contract as incredulous and immoral and that the king would never allow him to marry her.

And now, as she sat in the chapel with her head bowed, she struggled to finish her petitions because her mind wandered to Sir Devlin. He was prepared to leave at any moment to travel to Wisbech. She hoped and prayed he'd find answers there, but she wondered if anyone other than Edmond himself knew the depths of his lies and deceptions. Thinking of her uncle spawned images and memories that made her stomach churn, and her heart quicken, and she prayed that the investigation would be over soon. But at the same time, she feared the outcome.

At its conclusion, the best possible scenario would be that she would either be able to return to her father's estate or be left alone. She'd take the children, Marta and Benton, of course. It would be rough at first, but she was sure she could get the estate working again. There were lands to rent, and she could farm some herself. Or, if the king planned to return her childhood home to another of his barons, she could stay here. After all, she was Edmond's only heir.

And there was one option she had refused to think about because of the uncertainty and fear it carried with it—the king could marry her to someone else, and Edmond's lands would become her husband's. Additionally, the king could make her marriage even more advantageous and appealing to her betrothed and include her childhood home as well in the contract. Her title and lands would make some lord out there very wealthy. In this case, there wasn't a guarantee that the children would remain with her, and that possibility chilled her to her very core. In that event, she had to find a way for them to stay together and possibly live with Marta and Benton.

Rosalind took one last look at the cross that hung behind the altar, and she stood slowly. She turned and gasped slightly at the tall figure that stood in the door to the chapel. Once she realized that it was Sir Devlin, she smiled and said softly, "You can come in, you know. Praying is available to everyone."

"I fear that God may not welcome me here, milady," he answered back just as softly.

"And why would you think that, sir? God welcomes everyone into His house," she replied as she stepped toward him.

"The paths I've chosen haven't exactly been reverent."

"No matter," she assured him. "God knows your heart and your intentions. You see yourself as doomed, without a home...beyond redemption. But I see a very different type of man before me. I'm sure God sees that too."

"And what about you, Lady Rosalind? Your choices, the path you've taken, how do you see yourself? How does God see you?"

"I've spent many hours in prayer, Sir Devlin. I've done what was necessary to keep myself and the children safe, and I am at peace with that. God has seen all I have done, but He also sees my heart. I pray for His guidance and His mercy, without ceasing."

"And has it worked, the praying? Have your prayers been answered?"

Rosalind looked him in the eye. "I'm still waiting to find out."

She left the chapel.

Chapter Thirteen

He dressed in plain clothes and a worn cloak he'd
borrowed from Benton. He could not walk into the pub
clothed all in black, which would result in unwanted
attention, so the clothes were brown and tan homespun.
Benton fashioned a cloth eye patch to disguise his face
and trimmed his hair.

It was the best they could do, and Devlin hoped no
one would recognize him. As he and Alden prepared to
ride off, Ridley sprinted into the stable with a couple of
leather bags, which he attached to each of their saddles.

"From Marta. She said you might get hungry.
There's cheese, some bread, and dried apples," Ridley
said. "In case you're delayed."

The ride to Wisbech took only two hours, and
Devlin planned to return that same night. He wasn't
used to others thinking about his needs and wanting to
help, so he said nothing, but Alden replied, "Tell Marta
that the food is much appreciated."

Ridley stared up at the men, and looked so small
beside their mounts. "Safe travels," he said with a
wavering voice. "Please come back with…"

"Don't you worry for a second, Ridley. When I
come back, I'll have answers," Devlin said steadfastly.
"And I will come back."

Ridley nodded, and with that, the men urged their
horses into an easy canter and headed toward Wisbech.

****

Rosalind decided that staying busy was the best defense against the overwhelming worry and fear that welled up inside her and threatened to devour her sanity and her soul. She mentally drafted a list of things to do and moved from one task to the other as she tried to keep her hands and mind busy.

She worked on her spinning, and then she weaved a bit. She dusted and swept her bedchamber. Grim provided some relief for anxiety and allowed her to brush his coat with an old horse brush, but he eventually wandered outside to explore in the winter sun.

She made her way into the kitchen and half-heartedly attempted to cook the evening meal's pudding, but only scorched the milk in the pot.

"Kaylyn and Luella dropped their stockings in your mending basket, dear. Why don't you go sit in front of the fire and work on that?" Marta said kindly but firmly as she half-led, half-pushed her from the kitchen.

Rosalind sighed. Once seated, she realized sewing was the last thing she wanted to do. After three unsuccessful attempts, she'd managed to mend one hole when she heard Edward Kelley and his men enter the manor. Benton took their cloaks, and Rosalind's heart quickened as Kelley made his way to the great hall and to the other chair in front of the massive fireplace.

As he sat, a long, deep sigh escaped from the man. Rosalind paused her work on the tunic she was hemming for Ridley and waited for Mr. Kelley to speak. And then she waited some more. But he sat there, quiet, for a few moments and gazing into the fire. Finally, Rosalind couldn't stand it any longer.

"Good evening, Mr. Kelley. Were you able to get some clarity on this dreadful situation with Roland Kirkeby?"

The small man with the bulbous nose turned to her and sighed again. "I don't think I have ever met a more disgraceful excuse for a man than Mr. Kirkeby. The despot was drunk when I arrived. Can you believe that? He knew that a representative from the palace was coming to investigate his claim, and he showed nothing but disrespect upon my arrival."

"Of that, I am not surprised." She paused. "But did he have proof of a contract?"

"No. None at all. So, it seems that it's his word against yours, Lady Rosalind. And considering he was out of his mind on ale, I've decided not to pursue his claim any further. And this will be my recommendation to the king as well."

Rosalind almost jumped from her chair with joy, but she stayed composed. "I cannot say how relieved I am—I feel as if a weight has been lifted from my shoulders. And, Mr. Kelley, please know I am grateful for your investigation into the matter."

Edward Kelley gave her a slight smile, and she returned it with one of her own. Their conversation ended there. Rosalind and Mr. Kelley sat in relaxed amicable silence. After several undisturbed moments, the pounding of small feet was heard as Luella and Kaylyn rushed down the hall. When the girls saw Mr. Kelley, they both stopped short of entering the room.

Rosalind craned her head around the back of her chair and called out, "Girls, do come in. Catch me up on what you've been doing."

The children entered carefully, and Grim followed

clumsily. Enticed by the warm fire, the large dog then busted through the girls who were walking hand-in-hand, and plopped onto the rug with a grunt and a sigh. The canine gave Mr. Kelley no mind, and he started snoring almost immediately.

Kaylyn and Luella rounded the table, then stood in front of Rosalind. Kaylyn had a large hole in her woolen stocking and a smudge of mud on her cheek. Luella wasn't much better off. Her hands were dirty, and several pieces of hay were sticking straight out of her braids in several places.

"Girls, were you in the stable by chance? After you were told not to go there alone?"

Both girls started to shake their heads, and their mouths formed the word "no," but Rosalind held up her hand. "Choose your words carefully. Surely you will not shame this household with a lie in front of a representative from the palace sitting right here."

After a brief pause, the girls said in guilty unison, "Yes, Mama Rosalind."

"And what were you doing in the stable?"

"Ridley said the big black cat had kittens again. I didn't believe him, but he said there were three, and he got to play with them each time he went to the barn to do his chores. And that's not fair, is it, Mama?" Kaylyn stated with conviction.

Rosalind thought for a moment, "I agree. That isn't fair. But you're still not supposed to be in the stable alone."

"We wanted to ask someone, but everyone was busy, Mama," Luella chimed in. "We went out for a quick look, but we never found any kittens. I think Ridley was telling a story."

"And then you came right back to the manor, then?" Rosalind asked sternly.

"Not quite," Kaylyn answered after a slight pause, and then more words spilled out, "Luella went and looked at the body!"

Luella gasped and then reared back her small, skinny arm and punched her sister right in the shoulder.

"Luella! I'm shocked!" Rosalind exclaimed. "Why would you do such a thing?"

"What, Mama? I punch Kaylyn all the time. Especially when she tattles."

Rosalind sighed, rubbed her forehead, then looked back at Luella, her eyes wide and expression seemingly innocent. She heard a slight chuckle from Mr. Kelley. "Not that! But I will address the hitting later. Now tell me why you would want to look at a corpse." Rosalind demanded with all the authority she could muster.

"Well, Ridley tells us he hears Lord Edmond moaning when he does his evening chores."

"That's right," Kaylyn chimed in. "He says he's still moving out there too. Not a lot. But just a little."

"And I wanted to see if it was true. So after climbing in the straw to look for the kittens, I went to take a look."

Rosalind just looked at each girl, and she didn't know whether to punish the girls for disobeying or laugh, but Edward Kelley surprised her and joined the conversation.

"Oh, don't keep me in suspense, little one," Mr. Kelley asked with exaggerated but authentic interest, "Did you see old Lord Edmond move? Even just a little?"

Luella and Kaylyn moved over to Mr. Kelley's

chair. And with the snores of Grim, and the crackling of the fire in the great fireplace in the background, Luella and Kaylyn regaled the king's man with a glorious tale that included watching the wrapped corpse for at least an hour, throwing a few acorns at it, and finally working up the courage to poke Edmond's body with a stick.

"And did it moan? Or move?" Mr. Kelley asked.

Luella leaned forward and placed her small hand on the man's knee. With wide eyes, she whispered, with enough drama to sound frightening, "Yes, I believe it did."

Kaylyn nodded in agreement, and the older man placed his hand over his heart. "Oh my goodness! I shan't sleep a wink tonight!"

Both girls erupted into laughter, and the royal servant joined in. Lady Rosalind couldn't hide her smile and decided she would deal later with the girls and Ridley for telling such tales. She told the girls to get cleaned up for dinner, and they ran excitedly out of the room.

"Those two are quite entertaining and very clever," Mr. Kelley said when the girls had left the room. "I enjoyed their story immensely."

"It takes much of my energy and time to keep them out of trouble, but they are pure joy to me."

Mr. Kelley nodded as if he understood, and Rosalind wondered if he had children of his own. She wanted to ask, but Benton entered the room and announced that the evening meal would be ready shortly, and they both retreated to their chambers to change before eating.

****

The Boar's Head sat at the town's end and was all but hidden, concealed by large English oaks and a tall, unkempt hedge of vegetation. Devlin wondered that, if the walls could talk, how many crimes and secrets would be revealed. The structure boasted an exterior framed with sturdy timber beams and a thatched roof that sloped downward, while sagging dramatically inward at the same time. Moss and ivy clung heavily to most of the exterior and looked to engulf the structure come spring.

Above the entrance, a wooden sign, its letters barely decipherable, swung lazily in the breeze; its once-vibrant colors faded from years of warm summer sun and harsh winter winds and snow. Mist rolled in like a white cloak from the vast fields behind the pub and threatened to conceal the pub even more. Devlin took a deep breath, pulled his hood low over his face, and approached the entrance.

A burly man stood guard and eyed him suspiciously. "What's your business here, bloke?" he asked with a deep voice.

Devlin cleared his throat nervously, avoiding eye contact. "Just here for a pint."

The large man moved to stand directly in front of Devlin, crossed his arms in front of him, and replied, "Pub's closed."

Devlin looked past him and retorted, "Looks to me like ale is being served."

The doorman took a deep breath, leaned closer to Devlin, and said in a menacing whisper, "Look, you bloody bast-"

"Freedom whispers," Devlin interrupted, the words barely audible.

The man's stern expression softened as he nodded. He stood back and gestured for Devlin to enter.

The heavy wooden door creaked open, revealing a dimly lit interior filled with the hushed tones of secretive conversations. Devlin stepped inside, his senses heightened as he scanned the room. He quickly assessed the layout of the pub, how many men were present, and what his exit options were should he need to leave in a hurry. Worn wooden tables filled the space, and each held a flickering lantern that cast shadows on the wall. Surprisingly, the floor was covered with unevenly cut, flat stones, but it hadn't seen a broom in quite some time.

A few of the pub's patrons turned to watch him as he walked in, but no one moved to stop him. The atmosphere was thick with tension, and Devlin could feel the weight of the stares from the conspirators as they stopped talking. He wondered what secrets were being exchanged and what Lord Edmond's role was in it all.

The pub's noise faded as Devlin approached a table in the back. Two men entered the room through a door opposite the entrance. All the men in the room were quiet.

"Freedom whispers," the two men said.

The crowd shouted back, "Freedom prevails!"

And then a litany of curses against the king followed from the mouths of the men. A few mugs flew across the room, resulting in a new line of cursing from the barkeep, who must have been the pub's owner.

If he'd had any doubts about the opinions of this group about the monarchy, he didn't now.

A burly man with a bright red beard walked behind

the two men who had just entered and stood at the head of a long table. His sharp eyes looked at the patrons of each table.

The murmurs died down as the participants acknowledged the new arrival. Devlin felt a mixture of anticipation and trepidation as he took a seat at a small table crammed into the very back corner of the room. He was careful to keep his face concealed in the shadows.

The bearded man's gaze lingered on Devlin for a moment, suspicion flashing in his eyes, but then he turned his attention back to the proceedings. The room hummed with low conversation. Devlin listened carefully and caught snippets of various conversations—mostly complaints about the king and how more needed to be done.

Devlin strained to hear more of the conversation, and his ears quickly tuned to the betrayal around him. Soon, the red-bearded man, Robert, was his name, stood, and his voice rose above the others. He outlined a plan to steal resources from the crown to strengthen the Parliamentarian forces. He heard Edmond's name more than once as treasonous plans unfurled one after another.

It wasn't long before Devlin realized the depth of Capell's betrayal. Not only was he collaborating with the Parliamentarians to oust the king, but these conspirators didn't know that he was also playing them for fools.

From the ledgers, whose initialed entries now made sense, it seemed both sides were paying Edmond for information that benefited no one.

Devlin's hand clenched into a fist beneath the table

as he listened to the damning revelations. He struggled to maintain his composure when he learned how Edmond fed false information to the king, for which he paid handsomely, and then most of that money would go to Robert and his cohorts. Money was power, and funds bought weapons, information, and loyalty. Devlin was shocked to hear to what lengths these men would go to remove Charles from the throne. But at least now, he had proof of Edmond's collusion and betrayal.

As the meeting neared its end, Robert rose from his seat, and his guards flanked his position. Beads of sweat popped up across his brow, which eventually flowed down his cheek. However, as Robert prepared to exit, he paused, and his booming voice cut through the air.

"Who are you?" An accusatory outstretched finger pointed directly at Devlin.

All turned toward Devlin, and a chill ran down his spine. Robert's sharp gaze bore into him, and the room fell silent. Every breath was like an eternity as Devlin searched for the right words.

"I'm just a-a farmer," he stammered, trying to maintain his disguise. "I overheard talk of this gathering and thought the cause was noble. I wanted to offer my assistance."

Robert's eyes narrowed. The room seemed to hold its breath as Devlin awaited the man's response.

"I have never seen you before. How did you get in? After all, this is an "invitation only" affair." He laughed menacingly.

"I heard about your meeting here from an acquaintance of mine. Roland Kirkeby." Devlin exhaled but was poised to run. He hoped Alden had his sword and the horses ready. He had no idea if this man knew of Kirkeby or not or even if Kirkeby was a traitor like Capell.

Robert consulted with a few of the men at the table, and after a moment, said loudly, "This Kirkeby, I do not know. But my men say he is an associate of Lord Edmond Capell and not a very well-liked one at that. So, you're either a brave fool or a cunning spy. I will consider you the former as no spy would enter here and expect to make it out alive."

Devlin nodded, a sense of relief washing over him, and he stayed where he was, sipping a mug of ale as the gathering dispersed. He observed the conspirators as they left one by one. Robert finally made his way into the connecting room, and before the door closed, Devlin saw that he sat at another table. It seemed like there was another meeting—a private one this time.

Devlin stood nonchalantly, left the pub, and then immediately circled around to the back of the building, where he quietly inched his way over to the window of the room Robert had entered. He listened carefully. What he heard hit him like a fist in the gut. The men inside didn't talk long, and when they returned to the pub's main room for more ale, Devlin exhaled and moved quickly back to where Alden was waiting.

The weight of the information of Sir Edmond Capell's treachery sat heavily on his shoulders. The moon now hung low, casting a silvery glow on the few cobblestones on the path not covered with dirt. In the shadows, his horse pawed the ground in anticipation.

Devlin approached his friend. "Alden," he exclaimed in a hushed tone, "I learned all I needed to. Capell played a dangerous game. He betrayed the king.

He fed our liege false information, got paid for it, and then funneled the money to these blokes. And that's not all."

Alden leaned forward. "Not all? Goodness, man! There's more?"

With a satisfied grin, Devlin recounted the fabricated information Robert had concocted to deceive King Charles I. "Edmond was to tell the king about plans to assassinate a royal advisor by a foreign power aligning with their cause. But Edmond was also to tell the king that there were rumors of strife and division amongst the Parliamentarian leaders, to make them appear weak. Of course, with Edmond missing, this information never got to the king. What these blokes didn't realize was that Edmond was lying to both sides. He was taking money from the king to expose Robert and his group of traitors while taking money from them as well. He was feeding both sides incorrect information and pocketing some of the money. Both sides lost men because of Edmond's greed."

Alden's eyes widened. "This betrayal goes beyond what I could ever have thought Edmond capable of. I wouldn't have thought him smart enough to pull off such a scheme," he whispered, clenching his jaw in anger.

"Yes, and we can use this to expose Capell's true intentions. But here's the worst part. These traitors think that Lady Rosalind fully supports their traitorous plans. Edmond gave them money. Rosalind's money! If these idiots kept records, Lady Rosalind would be directly tied to this faction. We must get back to the manor house immediately. Kelley must return to the palace as soon as possible."

Alden nodded and moved to mount his horse, but then stopped with one foot in the stirrup. "Hold, just a second. Lady Rosalind doesn't have any money. If she did, she'd have gotten away from Edmond long ago. Or, at the least, not be dressed in rags all the time."

"You are correct, friend. This has been done without Rosalind's knowledge, but now she could be charged with treason."

The two men mounted their steeds and reined their horses toward Capell lands. Hooves hammered the narrow road leading from the village as they galloped toward the manor house as fast as they dared.

Upon reaching the manor, they found the clerk still awake in the study, surrounded by Capell's ledgers and notebooks. Though it was late, his eyes were bright, and he rose from his chair when he saw them.

"Do you have news, Sir Devlin?" Edward inquired with a tone that indicated her expected news but with an undercurrent of genuine concern.

Devlin wasted no time. "Capell betrayed the king, and we have evidence to expose his dealings. He fed false information to His Majesty and used the funds to line his pockets, all while weakening the monarchy."

Kelley raised an eyebrow. "Evidence, you say?"

"Yes, now I know what many of the entries in the hidden ledger meant, what the funds were for, and who gave them to Edmond. Not only do I have evidence of his crimes, but we now know many had the motive to kill him, or at least make sure he disappeared."

"If this is true, we must act now," Kelley declared, his voice tinged with urgency. "His Majesty and the monarchy have never been in more danger. The plans of these traitors are much more sophisticated than I had ever thought."

Devlin and Alden exchanged glances. Both realized this information could clear any suspicion of Rosalind in her uncle's death, but there was still a chance she could be judged as a traitor. Devlin turned away, and instead of haunting, young, blue eyes and the terrified face of a father, now wide, brown eyes bore into his soul.

Devlin and Alden pulled chairs to the study table, and the three men formulated a plan to present the evidence to King Charles I.

****

Lady Rosalind awoke suddenly from her slumber. She was surprised she'd fallen asleep at all, and her neck was stiff from her position in the chair. The fire was but embers in the grate and the moon hung low in the night sky, casting a soft glow through the one glass window in her chamber. Once she got her bearings, she thought the sound that woke her was a door slamming. Had Sir Devlin returned?

Her heart pounded as she rose, stiff from the chair, and grabbed her robe. She opened the door to her bedchamber and only took a few steps when she saw Sir Devlin round the corner in the hall. Warmth spread through her body. She finally exhaled the breath trapped within her. He was safe. He was unharmed.

But then her gaze traveled up to his face, and her heart fell. His eyes lit up briefly upon meeting hers but then worry replaced the spark and he forced a slight grin to his drawn lips.

"Lady Rosalind," he began gently, "it's more than we thought. Lord Edmond was involved in treacherous dealings against the king. His actions put not only the monarchy at risk but also your well-being."

Rosalind's eyes widened. "Tell me. What did you find out?"

Devlin carefully explained the fabricated information Capell was feeding to the king that protected the Parliamentarians and provided them with funds to buy weapons, travel, and spread information to advance their cause.

"How could my uncle have given anything to these men? He hardly had any funds to spare. I know the king rewarded him for information about his enemies, but it wasn't much."

"He gave the traitors your money, Lady Rosalind."

"*My* money. How can that be, Sir Devlin? I've never seen a single coin from my uncle. Supposedly, the king has control of my dowry, but that will go to my future husband, not to me."

"Lady Rosalind, the king has been sending Capell a cut from the estate rents from your family's lands since you were brought here."

"Yes, I know, but…"

"What you don't know is that the king sent specific instructions each year that you were to receive a portion of that cut. You should have received these funds—or at the very least, Edmond was supposed to spend the money on your needs, clothing, your education, whatever you'd expect a lady to need. The money was sent for your care and upbringing. The entries in the first journal. So many I can explain now."

"Well, that never happened," Rosalind said in disgust.

"He's been using your money, Lady Rosalind. Your allowance has been given to the Parliamentarians.

Some believe you've supported their actions."

Rosalind was speechless.

"I need you to understand that the evidence against your uncle is damning, and the king may believe you are complicit in Capell's betrayal," Devlin said.

Rosalind's eyes welled with tears as the gravity of the situation sank in. "But it's not true! I never had access to any of this money the king allotted for me. How could he have done such a thing?" She shook her head at her own question. "Of course, he did it! How could I even think that he had a shred of morals in that wretched body of his? He cared for no one but himself!"

Tears of worry were now tears of rage. "He made my life miserable every moment he was alive, and now that he's dead, he still threatens all that I love. I could lose the children! I could be married off to Roland or to some other wretched man. And if I never saw Marta and Benton, I couldn't bear it." Rosalind's knees buckled, and she nearly fell to the floor, but Devlin caught her in his arms.

"You must know that I will do everything in my power to protect you. I will not let Capell's deceit ruin your life."

She held his arms tighter and then laid her head on his broad chest. The strong, steady beat of his heart calmed her.

"But what can we do? The only person who should be brought to justice is also the only one who can testify that I had no knowledge of my money being used to overthrow the monarchy. And he is dead!"

Devlin outlined the plan to expose Capell's treachery, emphasizing the need for Rosalind to distance herself from her uncle's actions. "We must act swiftly and decisively. Mr. Kelley left only moments ago. He is prepared to report to the king that you had no knowledge of your uncle's dealings."

"He left? At this hour? Mr. Kelley has turned out to be quite a surprise, hasn't he? I would have never expected him to come to my aid."

"It's your spell, Lady Rosalind. You enchanted me easily enough. I fear no man is immune to your charms."

"There was one man who never succumbed to my charm, Sir Devlin. One that never cared or loved me. And now his deeds stand in the way of my freedom and could ruin the lives of the children and Benton and Marta, too." Tears of frustration welled up once more.

"We will face this together, milady. Your uncle was the worst type of traitor—he plotted against his king, but also his flesh and blood. My blood boils thinking about him, and if I had him in front of me now, I would haul him to the chopping block and drop the ax myself."

Rosalind knew he would, and this realization comforted her. However, her worry for the children, Marta and Benton, loomed large still.

"You have to promise me, Sir Devlin. You have to promise me that no matter what happens to me, you will do whatever you can to ensure the children are taken care of. They come first, understand? I can't have them sent to a horrible orphanage or become street beggars…or worse, be sold into servitude. Can you do that?"

Devlin nodded.

Chapter Fourteen

Rosalind woke the next morning with heavy eyes and a heavier heart. She'd remained in bed long after the sun was up, and she pondered if claiming illness and lying in bed all day was justified in light of her circumstances. Her gaze wandered up to the ceiling, and there it remained as she tried not to think at all.

The sound of delightful screams and shrieks broke her reverie. She knew the children were up and most likely giving Marta fits in the kitchen. She knew she couldn't lie there any longer. She threw back the covers, and the cold air from the room invaded her warm sanctuary. A small gasp escaped from her mouth. She'd heard Ridley come in earlier and stoke the fire, but the flames had died since.

Rosalind donned her day dress, woolen stockings, and shoes, and not feeling like fussing with her hair, she combed it out quickly and fashioned a simple braid that fell across her right shoulder. A glance into her mirror revealed eyes that were swollen and puffy, so she splashed some cold water onto her face from the water basin beside her wardrobe. She then took a deep breath, and satisfied that she looked presentable, rushed downstairs and into the warm kitchen.

Despite the loud yells she'd heard earlier, the scene in the kitchen was calm and peaceful, and she now understood why. Marta stood with her back to the stairs and bent over the counter, kneading a large mound of dough, preparing it for its first rise. The fire in the hearth burned bright, and the iron stew pot was already suspended over the flames from the heavy trammel hooks and crane that swung in and out of the fireplace.

Marta had been extra-productive, obviously because at the table the children were looking awestruck at Alden. He held their attention so intensely that Luella's mouth was hung open, and her spoon, heavy with porridge, was suspended in mid-air. Devlin sat at the far end of the table, his arms crossed and a faint smirk tugged at his mouth.

"...the shrieks from the barn were so terrifying— I'll never forget that sound, I knew the stock were in trouble. I ran as fast as I could down the hill, but the snow and ice were packed thick and hard and I slid after only a few steps. And then I saw it as I rolled down the hill!"

Alden paused for dramatic effect, but Kaylyn couldn't stand the suspense, "Saw what, Mr. Alden? What was it?"

Luella, now with a mouth full of porridge, said loudly, her words almost indecipherable, "It was the bear! I know it was!"

Alden took a bite of a scone, swallowed, and returned to his tale. "You are right, little mistress. It was the biggest brown bear I had ever seen. Its mouth was wide open, drool dripped from each long fang, and it growled and howled like nothing I'd ever heard. As I slid toward my doom, the beast stood up on its back legs and was taller than I am."

Alden paused again, and all three children froze and stared, waiting for him to continue.

"The bear roared and I feared I couldn't stop my rapid descent down the hill toward the stable. I tried digging my heels in the ground, but the soil was frozen solid. I rolled over and used my hands to grab anything that would stop my slide into the jaws of death."

A huge sigh came from Devlin, and he rolled his eyes and started to interrupt.

Alden turned away from the children and addressed Sir Devlin. "I beg your pardon, sir," Alden admonished his friend, "this is my story to tell."

"That's right, Mr. Devlin!" Luella concurred. "Shut your yapper! Let him finish. I want to hear what happened next!"

Rosalind gasped, and said firmly but softly, "And that will be enough from you, Luella. I think we've heard enough of this tale for now. Besides, it's time for your lessons—past time."

The children groaned collectively, but they didn't argue.

"Finish your porridge, and I'll see you upstairs shortly."

Rosalind fixed her own bowl of porridge, took a chunk of bread, and slathered on some butter. The children, now finished, left the room and raced up the backstairs, laughing and making bets on who would reach the solar first.

"To have even a smidge of their energy!" Marta exclaimed. "I'd have the cooking and cleaning done by mid-morning!"

Rosalind laughed and nodded "I am with you, Marta! So why didn't you send one of the girls to wake me? You didn't have to manage them alone while I slept the day away."

Marta smiled and answered, "Oh, but I didn't. Sir Devlin and Mr. Danby entertained the children while I got their breakfast ready. The story was quite engaging, don't you think?"

"Yes, quite." She turned to the two men. "Truly, I appreciate the extra rest, but I don't want you burdened with taking care of the children. You have your own tasks to see to."

"I had promised the children a story, milady, and so I took the opportunity to amuse this special audience with a chronicle of my exceptional fearlessness when faced with impending death," Alden said.

Rosalind managed a smile, her heart warmed by the gesture.

"And I shall finish my account of this harrowing experience this evening if you allow, Lady Rosalind."

Rosalind nodded. "I don't think the children would have it any other way, Mr. Danby. And I look forward to the conclusion as well."

Devlin grunted from his place across the table, "I wouldn't wait in anticipation, milady. I fear you will be disappointed."

Alden gasped in feigned insult. "I won't sit for a minute longer and have my character besmirched by the likes of you, sir. I shall take my leave and suggest you not join the children and me after the evening meal. Your sour mood will put a damper on our evening's festivities." Alden then stood and bowed to Rosalind, kissed Marta's hand, thanked her for breakfast, and finally gave Devlin a salute as he exited.

Rosalind giggled. "The children will certainly miss Mr. Danby when you both leave. His cheerful mood is contagious."

"Yes, he should change occupations. I'll check to see if there is a need for a court jester when I return," Devlin replied dryly and shook his head.

Rosalind's small smile faded as she thought about Devlin leaving. She knew that even with the best outcome, he would leave Capell Manor and likely never return. "We will know what the king decides to do about my uncle's death and about me soon. However, Lord Edmond's corpse lies in the barn, and that alone is rather unsettling, so if there's no reason why we can't bury him, I don't see a need to wait any longer. Did Mr. Kelley have any objection to a funeral?"

"He did not. He studied the body and came to the same conclusion that I had. There wasn't anything there that gave us any clues."

"So, he also found nothing, then?"

"Nothing at all. So, how would you like to proceed?"

"We will keep it simple, and we won't waste time. I'll send Ridley with an announcement to the village. We'll have a short service in the chapel tomorrow and he will be buried in the family cemetery, next to his father."

"Are there any other relatives to notify?"

"No. My uncle and I are all that's left of the Capell line."

"Good, this matter can be taken care of quickly. Does the village have a priest?"

"Father William serves the local village, along with three others. I hope we can locate him. I would rather not have a delay."

"Agreed, but Edmond will keep. The weather will remain cool enough, and when Ridley goes to the village, he can find the priest."

Rosalind shuddered as she thought about her uncle's body lying wrapped securely in the stable, and she searched deep within herself to discover an inkling of remorse or sadness. But there wasn't a shred of sentiment for the man. In spite of the turmoil that had come with the arrival of Sir Devlin and Alden, then Roland's absurd claims, and even Mr. Kelley, who could play a pivotal role in her future, life at the manor was much calmer since her uncle disappeared. She prayed a quick prayer for forgiveness, but she was thankful he was gone.

"I will send Ridley to the village immediately following his lessons."

Marta chimed in, "What about a meal after the service, milady?"

"I don't think so, Marta. My uncle afforded us no special indulgences while he was alive, so I won't be planning a repast to honor his memory. He'll get a proper burial, and I think that is more than he deserves."

Marta nodded and returned to her work table.

Rosalind looked back at Devlin. "Is that too harsh? I know it's unusual not to have some kind of meal for the family, but it's just us and I really don't want the entire day overshadowed by a funeral."

"I think your plan is sufficient. A dignified but simple service. And like you said, you are his only family, and I don't think the townspeople will be lining up to see him laid to rest."

Rosalind gave him a slight smile. "You're not wrong there. I don't expect anyone besides ourselves at the service. Let me get to the children, then. I'm sure you have matters to attend to as well."

She left and climbed the back stairs.

****

Marta joined him at the table with a hot mug of cider. Devlin waited for her to speak, but she just looked at him with a slight grin on her face at first.

He couldn't bear her scrutiny, and finally, he asked, "What is it, Marta? What do you want?"

"I want to know your intentions for my Rosalind."

"What do you mean?"

Marta started to speak, but Benton suddenly appeared as if he'd been summoned, and he took a seat opposite Marta and leaned forward, closer to Devlin.

Has Benton been listening outside the kitchen door?

"Please continue, Sir Devlin. We'd like to know if your intentions are noble."

"Intentions? I don't have any intentions concerning Lady Rosalind except to complete this task per the king's orders."

An awkward silence filled the room, and Devlin squirmed in his seat. The realization that a frail old man and a portly middle-aged cook could make him anxious made him question his manliness.

"So that's it, then?" Marta asked gruffly. "So you'll be out the door, never to be seen or heard from again after this mess with Lord Edmond is done?"

"What choice do I have? She is a titled lady and heir to her father's estate, and this one. I have nothing to offer. It's laughable to even consider she could be my wife."

"So, you've considered marrying her?" Benton interjected.

Devlin froze, and silence filled the room again.

"You'd better close your mouth, dear, lest a bug fly in," Marta said softly into the quiet.

"I…I…" he stuttered once more but then gained his composure. He thought of telling the inquisitors he faced an outright lie but he knew they would see right through it. "It could never happen, ever. But yes, I am quite fond of Lady Rosalind, and I've wondered many times if a life together would work."

Marta and Benton leaned back in their chairs and smiled at him.

"But it's a fairy tale. The king would never allow it, and Lady Rosalind would do better to find a man who could support and provide for her as a woman of her station deserves. I am not that man."

"I am a woman of faith, Sir Devlin," Marta said, "and I believe that God above will work this out. Where there is faith and love, there is hope."

Devlin appreciated Marta's kind words, but it was all a dream to stay here, live with Rosalind and the children, and own an estate.

"I disagree," Benton said strongly. Then, with his wrinkled and gnarled hand, he grasped the edge of the table and stood. Before he turned to leave, he said with conviction, "I think you are the perfect man for Lady Rosalind."

Devlin sat speechless, as the ancient butler tottered from the room.

****

Rosalind entered the solar and was surprised to see Kaylyn helping Luella with her letters and Ridley hard at work reading. The children looked up and smiled as she entered, but then Luella's little face fell when she sat at the table.

"Your cheeks look red, Mama. Do you feel sick?" the child asked.

Before she could answer, Kaylyn said, "Oh my goodness, you do. Shall I tell Marta you need something for a fever?"

Rosalind knew her face was flushed. Being in close proximity to Sir Devlin left her feeling warm all over. She had felt his gaze follow her up the stairs, and the heat rushed to her face. She wanted to run over to the shuttered window and thrust her head outside to cool herself, but the children might find that behavior odd.

The girls were very sensitive to illness, knowing they'd lost their mother to a fever, so instead, she said, "I feel just fine. Please don't worry. I don't have a fever. Here, feel my head and see for yourself," she said calmly and leaned over the table.

Each child felt her forehead and was satisfied she wasn't succumbing to illness.

"You've been busy, I see. Ridley, are you having trouble reading any of the words in that book? And Kaylyn, was Luella able to name all her letters?"

The children informed her of how well they had been doing, and the rest of their morning was spent reading and doing sums. Then, the girls practiced their stitches while Rosalind worked at her loom.

Ridley sat beside her on the floor and wound several lengths of yarn for her to use but looked up suddenly after the third ball and asked, "Is Lord Edmond being buried tomorrow, milady?"

"Yes, he is, Ridley. Tomorrow, there will be a brief graveside service, and he will be laid to rest next to his father in the family plot beside the chapel. When you're done, I'd like you to ride to the village and inform Father William he is needed here tomorrow at 11:00. Can you do that?"

"Yes, milady, I can. And do you know what happened? Was he killed, or was it an accident?"

Rosalind thought for a moment, unsure of how much to tell the children. After taking a breath, she decided to tell them the truth, but an abbreviated version at that.

"Sir Devlin discovered that Lord Edmond was collaborating and helping men who seek to overthrow the king. Landing up in the bog could have been an accident, but someone didn't want him to be found, that is for certain. Mr. Kelley believes there was some foul play involved, and that is what he's going to tell King Charles. And also that Lord Edmond was conspiring with his enemies."

"What do you think the king will do?"

"I'm not sure, Ridley. But I know that Sir Devlin is his loyal servant, and the king trusts him completely. He will listen to Mr. Kelley when he reports Sir Devlin's findings. I believe he will rule fairly in this matter. And Sir Devlin is prepared to testify to what he's found too." Ridley listened to her, but worry etched in his young face nearly broke her heart. "But for now, you must go to the village and find the priest."

Ridley paused for a moment and seemed to ponder the situation. Then, with a nod, he stood and left the room. Rosalind sighed, and her heart broke for Ridley. Being the oldest, he understood what could happen to all of them now that Edmond was gone. The girls, however, were not aware that their future hung in the balance. She sat frozen in fear for a second when she thought what could happen to Kaylyn and Luella, and her stomach rolled.

She closed her eyes, said a silent prayer, and willed her stomach to calm. She refused to give up and relaxed after a few deep breaths. She knew Devlin would keep his promise.

She looked up at the beautiful girls before her and forced a smile, "Come, girls, show me your work, and then I'm ready to bind off my work here. I'll show you how."

****

"Hand me that nail. It's by your left foot, man."

Devlin looked down at his foot and couldn't see the nail.

"It's right there."

Devlin scooted his foot slightly to the left and saw the iron nail head mostly covered in straw. He bent down, retrieved it, and handed it to his friend, who straddled a wooden beam that spanned the width of the hall. Alden worked to repair many broken support boards and some of the stall doors each day. After all, Benton couldn't climb up to the rafters, and neither could Ridley.

"Someone built this right. There's excellent craftsmanship here. No shoddy work at all. It's a shame that it's been left to ruin."

"Yes, the former lord, Lord Miles Capell, never did anything half-assed."

The comment came from Benton, who was working further back in the stable.

Devlin joined Benton where he was working. The old man was making a burial coffin. Devlin wondered if he should be touched by the old servant's loyalty to the family he faithfully served, or shocked that the man would waste time building a coffin. Edmond deserved to be rolled into a hole and nothing more.

"What are you doing, Benton? Why are you making a box for Edmond? I applaud your loyalty, but he doesn't deserve your efforts."

Benton looked at Devlin and then slowly turned, and his small, careful steps took him to a pile of planked lumber. Benton reached for a long plank, and Devlin stood to assist the man with the heavy piece but stopped. Benton lifted and carried the plank easily. And although he still moved as slowly as a snail, he carried the board to his workbench and placed it on the piece he was working on.

Benton turned to Devlin and said in a sad voice, "He wasn't always the man you came to know through your investigation here, you know. The Capell name was once one that commanded respect across the region and even favor from the monarchy. Why, young Edmond and our king were close friends. I had to rescue those two quite often from many careless choices when they were still in short pants, I tell you."

"King Charles, as a boy, was often here? At Capell manor?" Devlin asked.

"He certainly was. The boys were close, just as Lord Miles and King James were before them."

Devlin was shocked. He knew that Charles trusted Capell, but now he knew how far back their relationship went.

Benton picked up a large mallet and rigorously hammered the wooden nails into the board and again. When he was finished, Devlin asked, "So what changed him?"

Benton thought for a moment. "It wasn't only one event that changed Edmond. I think it started when he lost the love of his life. Not his wife. He never loved her. But there was one before her. He wanted her in the worst way. And the feelings were mutual. She brought out the best in Edmond. But her life ended tragically in an accident. He was never the same after she was gone."

Devlin could not conjure any version of Edmond who could ever love anyone that deeply.

"And there was a horrible argument with his father not long after. I was not privy to all the details, but I know Miles never truly trusted Edmond after that incident. And when Lord Miles passed away, Edmond continued making poor choices, with his money…and his life."

Benton turned away from Devlin to pick up a hammer, and as he fastened the planks together, his face remained sad and drawn. Devlin watched him for a moment and then left him with his memories. He hoped that for Benton's sake, he'd reminisce on Edmond in his younger years and have comfort.

Chapter Fifteen

Rosalind woke when the breaking dawn's shafts of sunlight peeked through the shutter cracks in her chamber's eastern window. She knew she should get up and move, but her body felt heavy, and her mood gray despite the promise of a sunny winter day.

The fire in her room had not been fed, and only a few embers burned in the hearth. Ridley had not made his rounds this morning. She propped herself on her elbows and listened, but she heard nothing.

She wasn't worried. The children were most likely still sleeping as Alden kept his promise and, after dinner, had told the conclusion of the story he'd begun that morning. Many more tales followed. The children were delighted with each telling, and she didn't have the heart to send them to bed. It was well past midnight before Devlin carried Luella to bed, and a very sleepy Kaylyn followed. She smiled because, for just a little while, she'd forgotten about her worries, and the cloud of fear and uncertainty lifted.

Rosalind somehow found the will to get out of bed, threw back the covers, and yelled, "Kaylyn! Luella! It's late and you must get up. Come now, and get dressed."

She heard a few groans from the connecting room. Luella entered her chamber. Her eyes were half closed, and her hair was sticking up all over her head.

Yawning, she asked, "Do we have to get up now?"

Kaylyn made her appearance, and while looking just as disheveled as her sister, she said, "Of course we do. We've got to put Lord Edmond in the ground."

"Kaylyn! We don't…," Rosalind scolded. She was going to lecture the child on respectfully speaking about the dead but then stopped. She couldn't think of anything to say about Lord Edmond that warranted reverence on the day of his burial.

Instead, she bent down in front of the girls and gathered them in her arms. "Kaylyn is right. Today, Lord Edmond will be buried in the churchyard beside his father and his father's father. And while I am not sorry that he is dead and gone, and I know you both aren't either, I still expect you to behave accordingly. We won't have lessons today or do our chores. We will stay calm and quiet and spend today in peaceful reflection and prayer."

Both girls looked at her wide-eyed but nodded and promised they'd be on their best behavior. Rosalind's heart nearly burst with love for these girls.

The calm and quiet lasted less than an hour.

The morning scene in the kitchen was chaotic. Marta stood at her work table, her rolling pin held high as she scolded the children.

"Kaylyn, finish your bread. I'll need some help here when you're done. Ridley! You and Luella, stop running! And for heaven's sake, get the dog out of my kitchen!"

Ridley ran through the kitchen with a small length of rope trailing behind him, which Grim was happy to chase. Behind the dog darted Luella, squealing with delight with the game. Rosalind sighed. Ridley's face was smudged with soot from stoking the fires and it seemed he'd been to the barn already too. An unidentifiable substance ran down his pants leg. Rosalind wasn't sure what it was, and she didn't want to know.

She turned her attention to her girls. Kaylyn was content to eat her breakfast, but Luella's plate was practically untouched, and her neatly braided hair was rapidly becoming undone. Rosalind sighed, but she wasn't angry.

"Children!" she called, but the melee continued.

"Luella, Ridley!" she barked out, this time a bit louder.

But still, the play continued.

She took a deep breath, ready to yell this time, but Devlin entered, accessed the situation, stuck two fingers in his mouth, and let loose with the loudest whistle she'd ever heard.

All movement, even Marta's wagging rolling pin, stopped, and Devlin said sternly, "Ridley, Luella, Kaylyn! Listen to your lady."

Luella and Ridley froze and were startled into silence. Kaylyn, who hadn't been doing anything to start with looked at Devlin and grinned mischievously like she relished the thought of her sister getting into trouble. And Rosalind wasn't going to waste the opportunity.

"Ridley, wash your face and then change your pants. Father will be here shortly to discuss the service, and you must look presentable. Luella, come here and let me fix your hair again. Kaylyn, you're dawdling. Finish your meal and help Marta. Come, children, there's much to do, and we are behind."

The children sprang into action, and soon the

kitchen was calm again.

Joining Devlin at the table after he'd prepared himself a plate, Rosalind smiled and thanked him. "You'll have to teach me how to whistle like that. It was very effective."

Devlin grinned "Yes, very effective for getting the attention of men, children, and animals of all kinds. However, I have found that girls have difficulty mastering this particular whistle technique. Perhaps we should get you a bell that you can ring loudly when the children are frolicking." He winked.

She blushed. Her attraction to this man grew each day. "I am not sure a bell would be nearly as effective. The priest will arrive shortly. Uncle will be laid to rest, and that horrible task will be over. I know that we need word from King Charles and his rule on the matter of his death, but I am optimistic that this will all soon be over."

"I agree. However, there is still one uncertainty that I wish I could resolve. Who weighed Edmond down in the marsh? I mean, what is the point? If anyone found his body, the death most likely would have been ruled an accident. And nothing was stolen, so there was no evidence of a crime."

Rosalind stared down at the table for a moment. "Do you think that the king will consider this and not put the matter to rest?"

Devlin shook his head, "I do not know. The king is often unpredictable. I dare not try to predict his actions." He reached out and covered her hand in his. "I will see you in the churchyard." And with a nod, he abruptly left the kitchen.

Rosalind wanted to scream at him to stop, to stay

with her, to take her hand, and never let go. His touch quieted the anxious thoughts in her mind and slowed her racing heart.

But that would not happen. So, she took a deep breath, said a quiet prayer, and rose from the table.

"Marta. I will be in the chapel."

****

Rosalind hadn't prepared the church for a service. Dry leaves that had blown in with winter winds accumulated in the corners, and the four wooden benches needed to be wiped down. The altar, however, was dusted and neat. Rosalind saw to that herself.

Edmond never frequented the small chapel; as the years passed, the priest came less and less. No, Edmond would not have wanted a funeral mass, and so she hadn't planned one.

Rosalind moved out to the cemetery and breathed a sigh of relief. A large hole now existed where there had been grass. She was grateful. Benton was too old to complete such a chore, and she'd not made arrangements with any of the villagers to complete the task. Alden and Devlin dug the hole without being asked and without complaint.

The next hour passed quickly. Father William arrived and he sought to comfort her.

"Lady Rosalind, please accept my deepest sympathies on the loss of your uncle."

The priest knew well the kind of man Edmond was, but still, he went through the motions as he would have with any grieving family. "Do you have any special requests for today's Rite to Committal?"

"No, Father, I just want it done quickly."

Father William nodded.

The children, herded by Marta and Benton, arrived, and Rosalind was surprised to see that all three were clean, their hair tidy and combed, and their clothes were tucked, buttoned, and orderly. The children stood beside Rosalind, Marta, and Benton, who flanked her other side. Father William stood at one end of the large hole with his Bible in his hand.

Once everyone was in place, Devlin and Alden carried the coffin out to the grave. Per her wishes, the service was completed in just a few minutes. Father William asked if anyone wished to say any words before the closing prayer, but everyone remained silent. Father William prayed, and Devlin and Alden lowered the coffin to the ground.

"You are welcome to come to the house for your mid-day meal, Father," Lady Rosalind politely said.

The priest agreed readily.

"Benton, you crafted a coffin for his burial. You shouldn't have done that. And you added the family crest," she scolded gently

"No, I probably shouldn't have milady. But his father had a proper burial, and his father before him. I was there both times. It just seemed the right thing to do."

Rosalind squeezed his hand.

The children watched Devlin and Alden as they shoveled dirt into the grave and even pitched in to help by scooting dirt with sticks they'd picked up.

Rosalind joined the men at the grave. "Children, let's go now. Marta has our meal ready, and you'll need to wash." She turned to Devlin and Alden. "I cannot express my gratitude enough for your help today. Please join us for the meal. I'll have Marta and Benton wait to serve until you get there."

****

Father William entered the manor with a spring in his step and a contented sigh, the solemn mood of the funeral behind him and the promise of a hot meal drawing him forward. Marta, though she was told not to make a large repast, outdid herself once more. The buffet held a large platter with a plump roast duck, baked and browned to perfection, small baby potatoes, honey glazed carrots, and sweet parsnips.

Rosalind, the priest, Devlin, and Alden took their seats at the table, and Benton arrived to fill their glasses. Because the meal was served on the buffet, each of them took turns filling their plates. Once they were all seated, Rosalind took her first bite of food for the day.

"And what of the investigation, Sir Devlin? Do you know any more about Edmond's killer?" Father William asked.

Rosalind nearly choked on her mouthful of food.

"Father, we still aren't sure if Sir Edmond's death was because of foul play, but the answer is no, we have not learned anything new. I have reported my findings to the king, and he will rule on the matter."

"I certainly hope that this terrible business can soon be put to rest. For your sake, Lady Rosalind."

"Agreed, Father. We are all ready to move on. This entire ordeal has proven to be quite worrisome."

The luncheon continued without incident, and Father William soon took his leave.

"Please do not hesitate to call for me, Lady Rosalind," he insisted. "I was never invited here when Lord Edmond was alive, but I am here for you and your household."

"Thank you, Father. I am grateful, and I am sure I can benefit from your advice."

The sound of approaching hooves interrupted the priest's departure. Rosalind and Devlin stepped outside to see a rider, cloaked in the king's red and gold silks, dismount and approach with urgency.

"Lady Rosalind, I bear a summons from His Majesty King Charles," the messenger announced, handing her a sealed parchment. "You are to appear before the king to answer questions regarding the death of your uncle, Lord Edmond."

Rosalind's heart sank as she broke the seal and read the summons.

Devlin, seeing her distress, stepped closer and read the document over her shoulder. "King Charles is impatient. We must leave immediately," he said.

Rosalind's mouth hung open.

Leave now? Go to court?

Her heart pounded wildly in her chest.

Marta and Benton appeared at the door and immediately rushed to Rosalind's side.

"Marta, I've been summoned. Sir Devlin says we must leave now."

Marta grabbed her hand and led her inside, "I will pack some food to take with you. You go upstairs. You are already wearing the best dress you have, and that will have to do for your audience with the king."

Rosalind stood frozen. The implications of what was happening finally hit her.

The king. Questions. Judgment.

Rosalind's world spun, and she swayed on her feet. Devlin rushed to her side, and he took both of her hands in his.

"Rosalind," he said softly.

She would not meet his gaze.

"Rosalind. Look at me," this time, he commanded gently but firmly.

She looked into his dark eyes.

"I will be with you the entire time. I will not leave you. You can do this. I promise you, I will do everything I can to ensure you are treated fairly."

And again, his presence calmed her. She held onto him desperately, and soon, her breathing calmed. She looked past him at Marta, nodded, then left the entry to go upstairs and collect her belongings.

****

Benton watched the last of the Capell line disappear around the corner. He turned to Devlin and said solemnly, "I have served this house for many decades, Sir Devlin. I took care of Lord Edmond and his father before him and as a child I helped my father serve the Capells before them. Edmond was not who he should have been or could have been. But there is one thing that I am certain of." He paused for a moment.

Devlin had never heard him speak so many words.

"Lady Rosalind is the finest, most loyal, and strong Capell ever to grace these halls."

Devlin nodded, but Benton was not finished.

"You will do all in your power to bring her back safely, no matter what, I know that. But if you find the king's judgment not going her way, I want you to give him this." Benton reached into his pocket, and gave him an object.

It was a ruby the size of a penny.

Devlin first wondered where Benton got such a

valuable jewel, but he decided he wouldn't ask. Benton was full of surprises. Instead he said, "This gem is impressive, Benton, and worth more than I will ever have, but it wouldn't be enough to bribe the king."

Benton chuckled. "Oh, it's not a bribe, Sir Devlin. The king will know what it is. You give him that and tell him what I said about Lady Rosalind."

Benton then gave him a slight nod and left. Devlin held the precious jewel, wondering what secrets Benton held in his ancient mind.

Rosalind rushed down the stairs carrying a satchel, and Kaylyn and Luella trailed behind her. Marta and Ridley emerged from the kitchen with a sack and a full water skin. Devlin took both.

Rosalind showed no anxiety in front of the children. She bent down and kissed each girl on their foreheads. Ridley, too old and 'manly' for kisses, accepted a warm hug from his lady.

"Now, children, I will be back the day after tomorrow, most likely. You are to be on your best behavior." Then she stopped. "No, not your best behavior. I expect you to surpass your normal standards and expectations for yourselves and be even better."

Devlin chuckled to himself.

"You help Marta and Benton and do whatever they ask. And Mr. Alden is staying behind. I'll be informing him that I expect a full report when I return. Do you all understand?"

The children nodded, solemn. Rosalind gave Marta a quick hug, then she and Devlin exited the manor. Alden met them outside, their horses saddled and ready.

Devlin gave Rosalind a leg up onto her mare, and he strapped her satchel to the saddle. He secured the food and water skin to his own saddle and mounted effortlessly.

Alden looked to the sky. The sun no longer hung overhead. "If you ride swiftly, you'll arrive at the castle by midnight."

The weather was cold but clear, and travel by moonlight would have to suffice.

"Alden, keep everyone safe," Rosalind said, almost pleading.

"You have nothing to worry about there, Lady Rosalind. I will keep the children busy and regale them with more stories of my amazing bravery."

Rosalind smiled, and then they were off. She looked back over her shoulder at the manor house.

"Stop, Rosalind, I know what you're thinking. But you will return. I promise."

Chapter Sixteen

As Alden predicted, Devlin and Rosalind arrived at Windsor Castle at midnight. The air was now frigid, and despite her anxiety over what lay ahead the next few days, Rosalind was glad their journey was over.

Their arrival was expected, and Devlin was well-known to the castle guard. They passed through the gate and dismounted. Stable hands appeared and took their horses, and two servants rushed out to collect their bags. Rosalind inched closer to Devlin amid the strangers but then felt relieved to see a familiar face join them outside.

It was Mr. Kelley, dressed in a green velvet doublet, breeches, and shoes. The smudge of ink on his cheek revealed he was still working at this late hour. He gave Rosalind a quick bow and immediately barked out instructions to several servants as he led them inside the castle.

Rosalind took a tentative step forward and looked up at the grand royal residence that she'd never had the opportunity to visit before. Her father's descriptions paled in the reality of what was before her.

Torches lined the road and fires burned in the two watchtowers that faced the direction they'd traveled. Through the dark, sprawling stone walls and multiple turrets were lined with wisps of fog. The castle was an imposing presence atop a hill. As she was ushered inside, she looked behind her as she crossed over the threshold. She could see the moon's reflection on the River Thames in the distance.

While the exterior of the palace stood as a commanding presence and announced the power of the monarchy, the interior was warm, luxurious, and welcoming. Her mouth dropped open as she viewed the grand hall she'd entered. The upper panels of the walls were lined with large tapestries depicting battles and several ancient emblems and banners of ancestors past. Closer to eye level, portraits of the English countryside and prized fox hounds hung at regular intervals on the vast walls. The floors in the entry were polished stone, perhaps marble, and everything glistened and shined.

Rosalind barely had time to take in the splendor as Mr. Kelley walked and spoke fast.

"The king will appreciate your promptness as he has grown most impatient with this matter. Tonight, you'll be taken to your rooms. There, you can wash up and sleep. Come morning, you will break your fast in your chamber and then be brought before the king when he summons you. Because this is a delicate matter, you will not be allowed to confer with each other, or have any visitors. The king wants you to only speak to him while you are here. Is that clear?"

Devlin nodded, and Rosalind replied, "Yes, Mr. Kelley. I understand."

"Good. You will be escorted now to your rooms by Reginald and Mistress Agnes."

Devlin and Rosalind dutifully followed them up the left side of a double staircase.

"And Lady Rosalind, I have one question for you."

Rosalind turned around.

"Did young Luella report any more ghostly happenings at Capell Manor?"

The tension broke and Rosalind smiled. Mr. Kelley chuckled, winked, and left.

As she and Devlin ascended the broad, spiraling staircase, the glow from a large iron chandelier that held at least fifty candles illuminated the faces of the monarchy eternally housed in grand oil paintings. At the top of the stairs, Devin and Rosalind followed the servants down a smaller hall to the left of the landing. Her heart slowed somewhat when she realized that their rooms were directly across from each other, but her relief was short-lived. A guard stood tall and still at her chamber door.

Devlin must have seen the panic on her face and quickly commented, "He's here for your safety as much as the king's, Rosalind. The king has enemies, and if they think you're going to implicate or expose them, you could be in danger."

Rosalind hadn't thought of the situation in those terms.

But then again, the king thinks I support those who wish to see him dead.

"I'm right across the hall. I will hear you if you call for me," Devlin promised.

With his assurance, Mistress Agnes led her inside and shut the door.

"Hot water has been brought up, milady. And there are refreshments on the table."

To her left, a tray of fruit and cheese sat on the top of a dresser, along with a pitcher of water. By the fire and on the opposite side of the room, steam rose from a substantial bowl of water that sat on the dressing table.

Rosalind was too nervous to eat, but the hot water would wash the grit and dirt from her body.

Agnes looked at her, but unaccustomed to having a maid tend to her needs, Rosalind was left temporarily speechless. She finally managed a reply that she hoped was appropriate.

"Thank you, Agnes. That is all I require for now."

Agnes curtsied and exited. Rosalind took a deep breath and surveyed the room. The space was not overly large, but the furnishings were opulent compared to what she was used to. The large stone hearth boasted a carved mantle depicting a fox hunt, complete with a troop of horses and riders, several hounds, and the wily fox. A plush chair and a small side table beckoned guests to come, sit and warm themselves before the fire.

To the right of the door, a four-poster bed with thick velvet curtains that could be drawn around the entire bed to hold in the heat looked heavenly. Her satchel was on the bed. She crossed the room and retrieved her sleeping gown. She undressed and washed her body quickly. Covered now in goosebumps, she toweled off quickly, took her gown over to the fire, and dressed. Still chilled, she grabbed a blanket from the bed, wrapped herself, and sat in the cushioned chair.

Her gaze was fixed on the flames, and she pondered her fate. Tomorrow, she would go before the king and profess her innocence. He would believe her, or he would not. Once again, she felt angry that one man held her future and her safety in his hands. Tears welled in her eyes as she thought of the unfairness of it all.

Rosalind heard a soft knock at the door. "Come in," she said. She quickly wiped the tears that had escaped from her eyes and sat up straight in her chair.

It was Devlin. He entered, his hair damp, and the black wavy tendrils hung loose about his face. He'd changed clothes as well and wore black trousers and a loose linen tunic open at his collar gave her a generous glimpse of his broad, strong chest.

"I wanted to check on..." Devlin began, but before he could finish his sentence, she stood, dropped the blanket, and a gut-wrenching sob escaped her.

Devlin opened his arms wide, and she didn't hesitate. She ran to him, wrapped her arms around his body, and held him as tight as she could.

He said nothing as he returned her hug with one as tight as her own. She was crying in earnest now, and nothing could stop the anguish tearing through her body. Devlin picked her up, carried her to the chair, and sat with her on his lap.

He was patient. He rubbed her back and kissed her head as her body finally released the hurt, the rage, and even the fear she'd been feeling for so long. When the crying finally stopped, Rosalind sat up, now embarrassed she was sitting on his lap, and in her sleeping gown, no less!

"I'm, I'm sorry." She hiccupped.

She placed her hands on his chest and moved to stand up. He held her fast.

She looked into his eyes, and before he could say anything, she blurted out, "Devlin. I realized I may never see the children, or Marta, or Benton again." Her last words ended with a squeak, and the tears threatened to flow again.

Rosalind pushed harder against him, and he released his grip. She paced the floor, her tears now replaced with rage.

"And here I am again, my fate lying in the hands of one man. A man, a king I have never met. I know nothing of his character. I could be locked in the Tower within hours…or worse. Practically all my life, I have been under the rule of a man who despised me, loathed my presence, and even used funds from my father's estate to conspire against the very man who ultimately decides my fate. The irony of it! And I can do nothing, Devlin. Nothing! Do you know what it feels like to be powerless?"

Devlin's mouth opened to reply but she didn't let him.

"Of course you don't! You are a man! You are strong, you are favored by the king. And. You. Have. Nothing. To. Fear." Rosalind punctuated each word with a poke to his chest. She moved away from him, "You stand there, and you are confident, unafraid because you know that no matter what happens tomorrow, you will leave this place." She stood in the middle of the floor, shaking.

Devlin was quiet.

"I envy you," she said.

Devlin approached her carefully, as if she was a small animal ready to flee and he gently lifted her in his arms. He took her to the large bed, climbed into it, and sat her on his lap. Rosalind placed her head upon his shoulder.

He offered no assurances or empty words that promised her everything would be all right. He just held her there in the quiet of the night, the glow of the fire providing warmth and light.

Finally, her trembling subsided, and her breathing

calmed. Rosalind's eyes grew heavy, and though she knew it wasn't proper, she lifted her head and looked in his eyes. "Will you stay until I fall asleep?"

Devlin kissed her lightly on her lips, nodded, and drew a blanket over both of them

****

It was nearly dawn, and Devlin hadn't slept the entire night. The thoughts of Rosalind being jailed, or worse, hanged for Edmund's treachery infuriated him. Yet beneath the anger, a cold, icy fear gripped his heart: the fear that he was on the verge of losing the woman he had come to love.

Love.

Without a question, he now knew he loved Rosalind. The emotion was still foreign to him, and he wasn't sure he could even articulate this feeling. He stared down at her face, and longed to tell her that everything would be all right and that they might even leave for home this very evening. But he knew he couldn't. To do so would be a lie, and he couldn't and wouldn't do that to her. But he knew he would move heaven and earth to save her.

In his arms, she slept deeply. He liked to think it was merely his presence that kept her panic at bay and allowed her to sleep, but it was more likely just sheer exhaustion. The panic that ruled her just hours before hadn't left. She was able to push it deep down within her core and block it from her consciousness.

He carefully placed her in the space beside him and slid gingerly off the bed. She stirred and opened her eyes. There was only a moment of peace. Then she caught the coming dawn through the cracks in the shuttered window. Panic crept back into the depths of her eyes, and tears threatened to flow again.

"I have to go, Rosalind," he said in a calm but firm voice. "The guards know that I spent the night here with you, but they will remain quiet. However, it won't be to our advantage if your maid shows up and I am in your bed. I have to appear impartial."

Rosalind nodded. He took her hand.

"I am just across the hall. I will come if you need me."

He released her hand and walked to the door.

"I know you will, Devlin. I know."

Devlin was again shocked at the goodness she saw in him and the trust that showed in her eyes.

In the hallway, the guards barely acknowledged Devlin as he left Rosalind's chamber. If they had any opinion of his spending the night with a titled lady that was under suspicion of treason, their faces didn't betray their thoughts. Regardless, Devlin shot each of them a piercing glance for good measure, then entered his own room.

Just as Mr. Kelley promised, a meal was brought to his chamber. His appetite was nearly non-existent, but he ate. And then he waited. By mid-morning, he paced the floor, much like he'd seen Rosalind do before.

Stop your hand-wringing!

Finally, he heard a knock at his door.

A young man with a nasal voice entered his room and announced, "The king will see you now."

Devlin followed the man to the hall. The first thing he noticed was that the door to Rosalind's chamber was open, and her room was empty.

"Where is Lady Rosalind?" Devlin asked calmly, but his stomach reeled at the thought that the king might be questioning her without him.

A guard cleared his throat. "The king's man, Kelley, escorted her to the king's cabinet room."

"How long ago?"

"Not long, sir. Only a half hour or so."

Devlin was angry, but there was some small comfort that Mr. Kelley had fetched her himself. Devlin wasted no time making his way to the king's cabinet room. His escort had difficulty keeping up with him and had to run the last few steps to get ahead so that he could announce Devlin to his liege.

Devlin sighed but allowed the formality of his introduction before barging in. He noticed right away that Lady Rosalind was not there. The king and two of his advisors were the only ones present. There was no Kelley and no Rosalind, and he had nearly forgotten where he was. He quickly took two steps forward and bowed to his king.

King Charles sat behind a long, polished wooden table, the fire in the hearth casting flickering shadows across the room. Though slight in build, his neatly trimmed brown beard, and dark, contemplative eyes lent him an air of quiet authority and intelligence. Devlin was relieved to find the king dressed in more casual attire—a dark velvet doublet worn over a crisp white linen shirt, paired with simple breeches that seemed to soften his regal demeanor.

"Ah, Devlin. Come forward, please. It's been some time since we've had a chance to speak." He smiled.

"Indeed, Your Majesty. But I am happy to be able to be here and assist in resolving this unfortunate matter concerning Lord Edmund Capell and his niece, Lady Rosalind."

"No one wants to get to the bottom of this more than I and what I learned from Mr. Kelley about my so-called trusted and loyal lord shocked me. But I have to follow the trail, you see. I have to root out and punish anyone who would sympathize with those who seek to usurp me, even if that person is a pretty young lady."

"Agreed."

"I value your opinion, Devlin. Before the lady in question arrives, I must know your feelings on the matter," King Charles commanded with piercing eyes. "You were at Capell Manor for several days, conducted the investigation, and lived with Lady Rosalind. Do you believe she conspires against me?"

Devlin exhaled. This question he could answer truthfully with not an ounce of doubt. "No, Your Majesty, I am certain she knew nothing of Edmond's complicity with the Parliamentarians. Edmond's books and records showed clearly that she never saw a penny of the funds you sent for her care and upkeep. And the state of the manor house, the furnishings...and the way Lady Rosalind was dressed, you would have no doubts that Lord Capell hoarded all the funds, gambled them away, or sadly, provided for your enemies."

His liege sat in silence and seemed to accept Devlin's answer, but then he asked suddenly, "Did she kill him, Devlin?" He stood and walked around his meeting table and paced slowly across the room in front of his knight. "Mr. Kelley told me that Capell offered her as payment in a game of cards. And I understand, the night Edmond disappeared, he had been abusive to Lady Rosalind. What do you say? Survival is a powerful motive, after all."

Devlin watched his king's movement carefully as

he spoke. "I agree with your assessment of the situation, Your Majesty. Lady Rosalind's life with her uncle was quite challenging, to say the least. However, I found her to have a gentle spirit and not inclined to anger or violence. And I found no evidence that she was involved in Lord Edmond's death."

The king started to speak, but the door to the council chamber opened and Mr. Kelley, with Lady Rosalind on his arm, entered. Rosalind's face was pale as milk, but her head was held high and her steps sure and straight. Mr. Kelley escorted her to stand across from Devlin. He gave her arm a reassuring pat and then joined the other advisors at a seat behind the table.

Rosalind stepped forward. With a steadying breath, she gathered the folds of her gown in both hands and gracefully dipped into a deep curtsy. Devlin detected a slight tremor in her stance. Her head bowed, and her gaze fixed on the floor as the weight of the king's stare pressed upon her, but she held her posture. After a moment, she rose carefully and waited for the king to acknowledge her.

"Lady Rosalind, do you know why I called you here today?" His words were not necessarily unkind, but the lack of any exchange of pleasantries indicated he meant to conclude this business as quickly as possible.

"Yes, Your Majesty. You want to question me about my uncle's involvement with traitors and also his death."

"I have questioned Mr. Kelley and Sir Devlin and heard their reports. However, while I may be convinced that you do not and have not ever lent your support to those treasonous bastards that threaten the continuation of the monarchy, I am not so sure that you are completely innocent in the matter of your uncle's tragic demise."

Rosalind's chest begin to rise and fall faster, and she nervously fingered the neckline of her dress.

"On the night Sir Edmond disappeared, did you and he have an argument that led to a physical altercation?

"Yes, that is true."

"And was this the first time he had struck you?"

Rosalind's gaze lowered. "No, it wasn't."

"Did he beat you often?"

Rosalind's chin rose slightly. "Depends on what you consider often, Your Majesty."

This king waited for her to continue.

"If you are the kind of man that considers a beating a day as often, then my answer is no. But my uncle was prone to drinking too much, and in my opinion, he hit me often enough."

"What of this Roland Kirkeby? Mr. Kelley tells me he won your hand in marriage in a card game. Why would my loyal baron negotiate the betrothal of his niece, the heiress to her father's estate and his, to an untitled scoundrel as this? It makes no sense!"

"If I may, Your Majesty," Mr. Kelley said, "It is my theory that Kirkeby knew more of Edmond's dealings with your enemies than we suspected. Perhaps Lady Rosalind was to be a payoff not just for a gambling debt, but for his silence."

The king nodded as he considered the plausibility of the theory. "Did you love your uncle, Lady Rosalind?"

The question surprised Devlin, but Lady Rosalind

didn't flinch.

"No, I did not."

"Did you hate him?"

"I hated what he did; I hated what he was. But I did not hate him. I pitied him."

"I believe you," the king said. "Did you kill him, Lady Rosalind?"

Lady Rosalind blinked once. Then again. "No. I did not kill him."

"Now this, I do not believe. At least not altogether."

It didn't seem possible that Rosalind could get any paler, but she did. Her breathing quickened once more. She turned her head his way and gasped, "Sir Devlin." Her voice was barely audible, then her eyes rolled back in her head, and she swayed.

Devlin barely caught her before she hit the floor.

"Take her out of here, Sir Devlin. Take her to her chamber, place her guards back on watch and then return."

Devlin's stomach sank as he carried Rosalind from the room. Once he had left her on the bed in her chamber, he immediately returned to the cabinet room. The king was back in his chair. He motioned for Devlin to sit in front of him. Mr. Kelley sat calmly.

"Devlin, I now have to disagree with you. You saw Lady Rosalind's reaction. I believe she may be guilty or, at the very least, involved in her uncle's death."

Devlin knew he had to choose his words carefully. "Your Majesty, I truly believe if she was complicit, that it would have been, at the very least, self-defense."

"If that were true, then she should have said so. I'm not an ogre, you know. I would have listened. But frankly, she looked nothing but guilty and had no words for her own defense."

"With the evidence against Edmond, I would think she would have done you a boon," Mr. Kelley said.

"Despite his treachery, Edmond would have been worth more to me alive. With the proper motivation, he could have led me to the leader of this plot against me and the throne. No, I cannot have members of my court killing each other. I am the law of this land and no one else. Everyone would be wise to remember that."

"And what of Lady Rosalind then?" Devlin asked.

"The circumstances are complex in her case. But I feel like a period of incarceration is justified."

Devlin tasted the bile that rose from his throat as feelings of rage and fear coursed through him.

"I will draw up the papers," Mr. Kelley said.

He turned his head slightly, and Devlin saw sadness in his expression.

"Just a moment, Mr. Kelley," Devlin said. He took a deep breath and knew that there was only one chance for Rosalind to get home. He reached into the inner pocket of his doublet. "Your Majesty, I have something for you. I don't know what it means, but I was told to give it to you if, after your questioning, you doubted the character of Lady Rosalind."

Devlin pulled out the ruby that Benton had given him. He placed it in the king's hand. The king looked down at the jewel and was silent. Beads of sweat formed on Devlin's brow.

He doesn't know what it is.

After what seemed like an eternity, Charles asked, "Where did you get this? I gave this to someone a very long time ago. But surely, he would have died by now."

Devlin was able to grin slightly. "A very ancient butler, known as Benton, gave me the ruby."

King Charles laughed, then paused, as if he was lost temporarily in the past.

"He said you would know what it meant. And Lady Rosalind is very special to him."

The king smiled. "The lady is free to go, Sir Devlin. You may escort her home."

Chapter Seventeen

"And he just said I could go? He didn't ask any more questions?" Rosalind asked, still not believing the ordeal she'd been anguishing over for the past weeks was finally over.

"That's exactly what he said. And Mr. Kelley will be back in Capell Manor in the upcoming weeks with details on how funds from your father's estate and Capell Manor will be distributed."

Rosalind rode in silence, still stunned. When she recovered from her faint, her first feeling had been intense fear. She had been afraid to open her eyes, fearing she'd be locked in a cell, but that hadn't happened. When her door opened, Devlin voiced the sweetest words ever spoken, that he was taking her home. She'd nearly fainted again, but from relief this time.

"Does the king intend to investigate my uncle's involvement with the Parliamentarians? Where did Benton get the ruby, and what did it mean? And does he plan to marry me off to some old lord who has outlived his last wife?"

Devlin smiled. "Slow down, Lady Rosalind, so that I can answer some of your questions. Yes, the king has tasked several of his closest advisors and a few hired men to investigate the matter of Edmond's alleged deceit. He will get his answers. And as for marrying you off to anyone, let alone an old man, he did not say. He only mentioned that he needed someone loyal to the throne living in Capell Manor to watch over those who he deems suspicious on the border."

"And the ruby? What did it mean?"

"Honestly, the king did not explain, and I didn't want to waste any time getting you out of there."

Rosalind nodded. She was thankful Devlin wanted to leave immediately. "I suppose we will have to ask Benton, then."

Rosalind was quiet. At the pace they traveled, they would reach home well before dawn, and she was conflicted. She wanted to be back at the manor with the children, Marta and Benton, but she also knew that Devlin would be leaving soon after he delivered her safely home. Dread settled over her, thick and heavy, and her breath hitched.

Devlin and Rosalind rode in silence as the sky darkened overhead, thick clouds blotting out what little light the moon provided. They were nearing the village of Aysgarth, and Rosalind's heart grew heavier with each passing moment.

"Let's stop for the night."

Devlin pointed to a small inn ahead. The sign creaked in the wind, reading The Sleeping Lamb, an old, weathered emblem that had stood the test of time.

Rosalind nodded, feeling sad but also tired.

Inside, the inn was warm and inviting. Flames flickered and danced in the hearth, casting shadows on the stone walls, and the smell of roasted meat filled the air. Devlin spoke briefly with the innkeeper, and the man behind the counter shook his head repeatedly. Devlin finally nodded in agreement with the man and offered her a small smile as he returned to her.

"Only one room was available," Devlin said quietly, glancing at Rosalind.

She saw the softness in his eyes, but it only deepened the ache in her chest. Rosalind no longer cared about propriety. Spending every last minute she had with him was all that mattered.

When they entered their small chamber, Rosalind walked to the window and stared out into the dark. She couldn't bear to look at Devlin, knowing what the morning would bring.

"When we return... you'll leave again. Won't you?"

Devlin was silent for a moment. She turned to face him, her heart pounding in her chest.

"I have to," he said softly, but she heard reluctance in his voice. "The king requires I report back to him. He'll have a list of men he wants brought to justice, Rosalind. I wish…"

"And what of me? What if I never see you again?" The words escaped her before she could stop them. She hated that she sounded weak, and she quickly turned away. Even though she knew he would eventually leave Capell Manor, she had pushed her feelings of dread to the furthest recesses of her mind. However, now she had no choice but to face the reality of him leaving.

Devlin crossed the room and gently touched her arm, turning her to face him. "I'll come back to you. I swear it."

She searched his face, her pulse quickening at the closeness. Before she could think, she leaned forward, closing the distance between them. Their lips met in a soft kiss, and Rosalind wished for time to stand still.

She never wanted to let him go. He raised his hands and framed her face gently as they lingered for a moment more. When they finally pulled apart, their foreheads rested against each other.

Devlin whispered, "I would never leave you willingly, you have to know that. The king has ordered me to come back. I cannot disobey him."

Rosalind believed him.

Devlin broke away from their embrace and secured the door. Rosalind fell onto the bed and closed her eyes as he blew out the two meager candles provided to them. She fell asleep in his arms, savoring the warmth of his touch, and for that moment, it was enough.

****

The pale light of dawn crept through the cracks in the shutters, a most unwelcome intruder. Rosalind knew she was alone. Devlin was already up, preparing the horses. She swallowed the lump in her throat, reminding herself that she had to be strong.

Their long ride to Capell Manor flew by in what seemed like only minutes. Upon their arrival, Ridley dashed frantically into the manor house. His voice echoed through the open door as he ran, breathless but excited, "They're back! They're back!"

Luella and Kaylyn appeared first, barreling down the hall and through the front door, their faces alight with joy. Still holding a dish towel, Marta rushed behind them, her eyes wide with relief. Benton emerged from the kitchens, bent and shuffling across the floor faster than usual. A wide smile spread across his wrinkled face.

Rosalind barely had time to dismount before Luella threw her arms around her legs, squeezing tightly. "I

207

knew you'd come back, Mama Rosalind!" she cried, her voice muffled against Rosalind's cloak.

Ridley brushed a stray tear from his cheek and grinned widely. Kaylyn wasn't far behind, though her expression was more reserved. She hugged Rosalind.

"We behaved just like you said," she informed her, her chin raised proudly. "Alden told us more stories too."

Rosalind laughed, though the weight of the past days hadn't yet left her. She stroked their hair, whispering, "Thank you, all of you. You've done well."

Devlin dismounted beside her, greeting Benton and Marta with nods. "All was well during our absence?"

"Indeed, Sir Devlin," Benton replied, his gaze lingering on Rosalind.

"Though I dare say the children missed their lady more than they let on." He gave Rosalind a knowing look before he turned back toward the house.

Alden appeared from around the corner and took in the happy scene. "I believe we did quite well keeping the manor going in your absence, right children?" he asked with a grin. "And only one small calamity for the duration."

"Mr. Alden!" Luella yelled, "We all made a promise not to tell. A pact, you called it!"

Alden dramatically threw his hand over his mouth. "I wasn't speaking of that calamity, little mistress. Now it is you who have revealed our secret!" He laughed. "Now, let us all go in and hear what Lady Rosalind has to report."

As they all moved inside, Marta ushered them toward the fire. "Sit, both of you," she commanded, her usual sternness softened by her relief. "You've been through a strenuous time for sure, milady. I'll have something warm brought right out."

Rosalind was near weeping. The weight of the journey and the strain of the king's court had left her needing the warmth and comfort that only home and Marta's cooking could provide. The children chattered happily around Rosalind, their stories and laughter filling the room. Although she'd been gone barely three days, the children had kept Benton, Marta, and Alden very busy. Once everyone was together around the great hearth, the room fell quiet, and everyone looked toward Devlin and Rosalind in anticipation.

Finally, Devlin announced, "The king has ruled that Lady Rosalind is innocent in the disappearance and death of Lord Edmond and also cleared her from any suspicion of, and any collusion with the Parliamentarians."

Marta gasped happily, and Benton let out a reserved but heartfelt hurrah. Both servants rushed over to hug Rosalind. Luella and Kaylyn, who didn't understand the importance of the announcement, still cheered along but then moved to the corner of the room and picked up their dolls. Rosalind was glad they didn't ask questions.

Alden, Devlin, and Benton sat around the table, where Rosalind joined them. Ridley pulled a chair up to sit close to her.

"Let me fetch the food and drink. Don't begin your tale without me!" Marta rushed to the kitchen.

The fire crackled softly in the hearth, and the girls chatted quietly with their dolls in the corner. Rosalind's body let loose a slight shiver as negative thoughts intruded into her contentment. When Marta returned,

Rosalind knew it was time to give a full account of what had happened at Windsor.

With a sigh, she said, "I know you are curious about my meeting with the king, and I have to tell you about something that was miraculous."

Marta sat and waited for her to continue. Kaylyn and Luella looked up from their dolls, and took a seat on the floor by her feet. Devlin leaned back in his chair; his arms crossed but his attention fully on Rosalind. Benton sat quietly; his weathered face unreadable.

"When we arrived at the palace, I was brought before the king the very next morning, just as expected. He had many questions about Uncle Edmond and what had happened that night. He was direct, and I could tell he wasn't sure whether to believe me."

Kaylyn's eyes widened, and Luella leaned in closer, her face full of concern.

"What did you say to him?" Kaylyn asked.

"I told him the truth, of course. But he was skeptical. You see," Rosalind continued, her voice lowering, "the king wasn't just suspicious of Edmond. He suspected that I had played a part in his death."

The children gasped, their little faces stricken with disbelief.

"But you didn't, Lady Rosalind!" Ridley exclaimed.

"The king needed to be convinced. And I was petrified! I thought for sure the king would throw me into the Tower. And I must admit," her voice grew softer, "at one point, it all became too much, and I fainted right there in front of him."

The children stared at her in shock, and then Luella broke into a giggle. "You fainted, like in one of Alden's stories?"

Rosalind laughed along with them, the tension lifting slightly. "Yes, Luella, you'll have to tell me who fainted in Alden's tales, but yes, just like in one of those stories."

"But then what happened?" Ridley asked, still on edge.

Rosalind glanced at Devlin, who gave her an encouraging nod. "The most amazing thing happened. After I fainted, Sir Devlin carried me back to my chamber. And when I woke, the king had sent word that I was free to leave. He decided not to pursue the matter any further. Benton, may I ask you something?" she said softly, glancing at Devlin, who gave her a knowing look.

Benton, sitting near the fire, nodded solemnly. "Of course, milady. What is it that troubles you?"

"I believe the king suspected me, Benton. I fainted and wasn't able to give him a full defense; I could feel his doubt. I was certain he would have me imprisoned. But my words didn't convince him to let me go." She paused, her eyes narrowing as she searched Benton's face. "It was the ruby, the one you gave Devlin. When Devlin handed it to the king, everything changed. He recognized it, and after that, he set me free. Benton, what did that ruby mean? Why did it make the king change his mind?"

Benton sat silently for a moment; his eyes distant as if recalling a long-buried memory. The firelight flickered across his face, casting deep shadows in the lines of his weathered features.

"The ruby, milady, is more than just a gem. It is a symbol of a promise made many years ago, long before the king was a man."

Rosalind leaned forward, captivated.

"When the king was just a boy—no more than eleven or twelve—he and your uncle, Edmond, were inseparable. Charles would often visit Capell Manor with his father, but like all young lads, he had a rebellious streak. One day, Edmond and Charles disobeyed their fathers and their nannies and left the castle grounds without telling anyone. The household staff searched the manor and the gardens, but no one found a trace of the boys. Charles's father was furious and ordered every man and woman to keep looking and not stop until they were found. I was a younger man then and often tasked with tracking down Edmond. I knew where he liked to play and explore."

He took a deep breath, his voice growing softer. "I found them by the river. It had rained heavily the night before, and the river was swollen and dangerous. The young prince—our king now—had slipped on the muddy bank and fallen into the current. Edmond struggled to pull him out, but the water was too strong."

Rosalind gasped, her hand covering her mouth.

"I didn't think twice," Benton continued. "I dove in after them. The current was fierce, but I reached the prince and pulled him to safety. Edmond, too. We were all soaked and half-frozen but alive. The prince—our king—was grateful, of course. He gave me the ruby as a token of his thanks. The ruby was from his signet ring and he asked me to promise not to tell his father what had happened. He didn't want anyone to know that he and Edmond had been so foolish." Benton smiled slightly, though it didn't reach his eyes. "The ruby was a gift, but it was also a symbol of a secret we shared.

And as I suspected, the king had not forgotten what had happened that day."

Rosalind was silent for a moment. "So... he let me go because he remembered you saved him."

Benton nodded slowly. "It's not often a king owes his life to a simple butler. But that day, I saved him. And perhaps in his heart, he knew he could trust you because I trust you, or maybe he thought to pay his debt to me."

Rosalind took Benton's hand. "Thank you, Benton. For everything."

Benton gave her a small, respectful bow of his head. "You're welcome, milady. I'm just glad you're home."

****

The rest of the day passed in unusual, almost peaceful quiet as the odd assortment of people at Capell Manor—servants, orphans, two mercenaries for hire, and one fierce-looking but gentle dog—settled right back into their routines.

The shift in the mood of the household was palpable. It was as if the manor itself breathed a sigh of relief. Where there were once shadows and darkness, now there was a home filled with laughter, warmth, and hope.

Even Benton, who was usually slow and intentional, moved with a lightness in his steps, and Marta hummed softly to herself as she bustled about the kitchen. Devlin spent the day watching them but didn't want to leave. He had never had a family, not one like this, anyway. But he knew this was not his world.

As the afternoon faded into twilight, Devlin could no longer delay the inevitable. He stood by the fire, his back to the room, and stared into the flames. "I have to leave tonight," he finally announced, his voice heavy with the weight of the decision.

The room fell silent behind him.

"You can't," came Rosalind's soft reply. "Not yet. Please stay until morning. Just one more night."

Devlin closed his eyes, every part of his body and soul longing to stay, be near her, and hold her just once more. But he knew he couldn't. The pain of staying, of lying next to her and knowing he would have to walk away in the morning, was more than he could bear.

"I can't," he said, turning to face her. "If I stay… Rosalind, it will only make leaving harder."

Tears welled in her eyes, but she stood tall, her chin trembling as she tried to compose herself. "Then don't leave," she whispered, but there was no demand in her voice, only a heartbreaking plea.

Devlin shook his head, stepping forward to take her hands in his. "I have to. The king will need me, and if I disobey his command to return immediately, it will not end well for me. You know that." His voice softened, and he gently squeezed her hands. "But Alden will stay with you. And Grim," he added, glancing at the large, protective dog who had become just as much a part of the household as the children themselves. "They'll keep you safe until the king decides what happens next."

Rosalind's tears finally fell, and she blinked them away, her hands gripping his tightly. "And what of you, Devlin? What if the king never sends you back? What if…" Her voice cracked.

Devlin's heart shattered. He cupped her face gently in his hands, wiping away her tears with his thumbs. "If there's a way for me to come back, I will. I promise you that. But you'll be safe here, Rosalind. You're the heiress now—two estates are yours. No one will dare harm you with Alden here and Grim by your side."

"Promise me again," she whispered, her voice breaking.

Devlin leaned down. "I promise." He met her lips in a brief kiss that was bittersweet. He pulled away, turned to Alden, and said gruffly, "Take care of them."

"You know I will," Alden replied.

As if sensing the gravity of the moment, Grim padded over to Rosalind, his massive frame brushing against her legs. Rosalind buried her hand in the thick fur at his neck. Then she followed Devlin to the door. After he mounted his horse, he looked at the manor that had come to feel like a home. Finally, he turned his mount and rode away. He didn't look back.

Rosalind stood in the doorway, her arms wrapped tightly around herself, watching him disappear into the twilight. Alden stood beside her, silent, offering the quiet strength she needed.

"He'll be back, milady," Alden said softly.

She wished she could believe Alden's words.

Chapter Eighteen

Rosalind cried herself to sleep. Her sadness bordered on despair and came with a dose of shame as well. After her visit with the king, she had so much to be grateful for. After all, she was cleared of any wrongdoing, and Edmond was gone. She and the children were safer than they'd ever been.

And she was wealthy.

As the heir to two estates that were at one time prosperous, she now had the means to support herself and her family. And if the king allowed, the attention of many influential suitors would soon come her way. She finally fell asleep thinking about the life she could have—one of balls and dances, visiting London, fine clothes, and never having to sweep or do laundry again. Her dreams should have been a comfort, but instead she was tormented.

When her eyes opened before dawn, she knew exactly what she wanted—and it wasn't balls, or fancy clothes, or a life of leisure.

I only want Devlin.

The tears welled in her eyes again, as the desires of her heart were like a mist that disappeared with the coming sun. She could not see the king allowing her to marry for love. He needed strong alliances, and a carefully arranged marriage with a fat purse attached to the deal was an effective means to that end.

"Mama Rose." It was Kaylyn. "Are you awake?"

She quickly wiped her eyes, "Yes, sweetie, I am. What's wrong?"

"I heard you cry out and I worried you were having a bad dream."

The child ran over the cold stone floor and jumped into bed with her. It was only a matter of minutes before Luella and Grim joined her in bed as well.

"I'm doing just fine, sweet girls. Don't you worry about me," Rosalind assured them as she stroked Grim's broad head.

The girls, content and believing her words of assurance, curled up beside her and quickly fell asleep. But she lied. She was far from fine as she tried to draw strength from the large dog and the two smaller bodies curled up next to her.

****

Loneliness weighed heavily on Rosalind, but another feeling began to emerge. It was power. Now she had choices. The estate was entirely hers. And until the king found her a husband, she would do her best to make the Capell lands profitable and the manor shine!

No time to wallow in self-pity. Staying busy will keep me sane.

For three days, she rose with the sun each morning and walked the manor's grounds, making notes on all that needed to be done to the stables, the animal pens, and the manor house itself.

"Alden," she said the morning of the second day after Devlin had left, "I want the estate to produce a quick profit. I may not have enough time, but I want funds for the children if I have to leave. I will not leave them empty-handed."

Before she'd left, Mr. Kelley surprised her with a small bag of gold coins. "This is for you, Lady Rosalind," he'd said. "A token from the king to replace a bit of what you've lost over the years."

Her hands shook when she opened the bag and gold coins glimmered from the bottom of the velvet reticule. She'd already hidden the coins away.

My family will not be left penniless.

Alden, always cheerful, stayed by her side and lifted her spirits with his stories and jests. He had recruited men from the village to start the repairs and even posted a couple in the guard towers at night. He'd visited the village and announced that there were lands to rent and jobs to be had in the spring to prepare the fields for planting oats and wheat.

"You've done well, Rosalind," Alden remarked one evening as they sat in the great hall, watching the fire crackle in the hearth. "The manor is coming alive again."

"Thank you, Alden. The manor looks better than it ever has." She thought of the tapestry Marta had completed and now hung over the mantle, and the rugs, now clean and repaired, warmed the floors.

"I wish Devlin…"

Alden placed a hand on her shoulder. "Devlin is a man of honor. I've never known him to go back on his word. If he said he would return, he will. But the king can be unpredictable. It could take some time."

"I know," she whispered, staring into the flames. "It's just… I feel as though it's been forever when it's only been a week! I am pathetic, aren't I?" She ended her sentence with a half-hearted laugh.

"You most certainly are not," Alden replied

emphatically. "You are in love, my dear. That is all."

****

Nearly a month passed, and Rosalind remained outwardly strong, keeping the children close and attending to the estate's demands. However, each night, she climbed into her bed and concentrated on thoughts of Devlin. Her fervent wish each night was to receive him in her dreams.

Some nights, he came to her in the hazy, ethereal dream world; his presence vivid, almost tangible, as though he'd merely stepped away for a moment and returned to her side. The dreams were both a blessing and a curse. She could almost feel his warmth, feel his intense stare, and sometimes reach out to touch him. She would awaken with a quickly fading memory that left her wanting more.

"The quick sale of the swine litter provided a tidy profit. I'll have enough to buy Ridley his first brood mare in no time at all, I think," Rosalind said proudly as she pored over the manor's ledger with Alden early one morning.

Alden smiled back at Rosalind's tired face. "That's good to hear. And we'll have several sheep birthing soon. We can sell them when they are weaned to provide more funds long before the fall harvest."

Their conversation halted as the door opened and slammed against the wall.

"Milady, a messenger has arrived from the king. Mr. Kelley is on his way to see you!" Ridley exclaimed, nearly out of breath.

Rosalind's heart beat so hard she thought it would lurch out of her chest. Finally, after so much waiting, the king's decision would be revealed. Would she be married off to some lord in need of a rich heiress? Would she be allowed to remain here or return to her father's estate? What would happen to the children? She couldn't say what fate awaited her, but one thing she was certain of—her future would be decided today.

Alden met her gaze. "Do you want me to meet with him first?"

"No," Rosalind replied, standing tall. "I will see him myself."

Her hands trembled slightly as she smoothed her gown and took a deep, steadying breath. Her entire life, her future had been controlled by others, but she was ready to face whatever came.

When Mr. Kelley finally arrived, she stood waiting in the great hall, her heart pounding in her ears. As the door opened, Mr. Kelley strode in with his usual briskness, but she saw his slight smile. Marta and Benton joined them.

Then time stopped, and Rosalind couldn't breathe. She blinked twice, not believing her own eyes. Mr. Kelley was not alone.

Devlin stood weary before her, wearing his usual black attire and ebony hair hanging just to his sagging shoulders. His shadowed eyes were focused squarely on her.

"Devlin…" Her heart raced.

Before she could move or speak again, Mr. Kelley stepped forward, his tone formal yet tinged with excitement.

"Lady Rosalind," he began, "His Majesty has made his decision. I am sure you are quite anxious to hear his ruling on this matter, and I am not one to make you wait. Shall we speak here?"

"Yes, please, Mr. Kelley. I cannot wait another moment. You can speak freely in front of Benton and Marta."

Mr. Kelley smiled in understanding. "The king recognizes that you are the sole heir to the Capell estate; however, he sees no advantage to the monarchy in granting you the Capell lands. He feels strongly that he needs this holding to secure the borders and monitor the king's enemies. In exchange for Capell Manor, however, you have been granted a rare gift."

Rosalind blinked in confusion. "A gift?"

"A choice," Mr. Kelley continued, his eyes gleaming with the weight of his message. "The king regrets the abuse you endured under the care of your uncle. And for that, he has now given you the power to choose your own husband. You may marry any man or no man at all. Your estate inherited through your father shall remain in your name—but he requires you to surrender all the Capell lands to His Majesty."

Rosalind's heart skipped a beat. The king was allowing her to choose! She was able to keep and would return to her childhood home!

"Any man? Any man at all, you say?"

Mr. Kelley nodded "Any man or no man, my lady. And that's not all. I will let Devlin share this next part."

Devlin knelt in front of her, his voice low. "Rosalind, I've come back to you, and that's not all. The king has released me from my duties. I am a free man."

Rosalind's breath caught in her throat, as her mind processed Mr. Kelley and Devlin's announcement.

"Rosalind, I want to marry you. If you'll have me, I'm yours."

All the waiting, all the fear, melted away in that single moment.

"I don't even have to consider your proposal, Devlin. All I've only ever wanted is you. My answer is yes!"

A slow smile spread across Devlin's face, and in that instant, Rosalind knew her decision had already been made long ago. The Capell estate, the king's plans, none of it mattered compared to the love standing before her.

Benton and Marta smiled from ear to ear and once again Marta wiped tears from her face. Alden clapped Devlin on the back and shook his hand.

Mr. Kelley bowed slightly. "Then I shall inform the king that the matter is settled."

Benton motioned for Mr. Kelley to sit, and they found seats at the end of the long table. Marta announced that she'd fetch wine to celebrate and retreated to the kitchen.

Rosalind and Devlin stood facing each other, smiling, but then her heart stuttered and her stomach fell.

"Rosalind, what is the matter?"

"Devlin, I must speak to you now. Alone."

Benton and Mr. Kelley were already deep in conversation. The couple left the great hall and quickly went upstairs to the solar.

Rosalind closed the door behind her and stood before Devlin, her heart pounding in her chest. She could hardly look him in the eyes. "You may not want to marry me," she whispered, her voice trembling.

Devlin's head tilted slightly, and his brow furrowed. He stepped closer, reaching for her hand, but she pulled it away.

"Rosalind, nothing could ever change my mind about you. I love you."

She shook her head, her fingers twisting the fabric of her gown at her neck, "You don't understand. You think you know me, but you don't. You don't know what I've done, Devlin. I... I lied to you. I've lied the entire time you and Alden have been here."

She looked him squarely in the eyes. There was no anger and no surprise. He started to speak, but Rosalind cut him off. She was unable to stop.

"You've known all along, haven't you?" she asked, her voice thick with emotion. "You knew I was there... when Edmond died."

Devlin was silent for a moment. He reached into his pocket and pulled out the delicate silver locket. He held it between his fingers, and Rosalind's breath caught in her throat.

"I found it," he said softly, "in Edmond's hand when I pulled him from the bog. I knew that you were there. You knew what happened to him, and you kept that from me. Yes, you lied to me, Rosalind, but you lied to protect yourself and the children. You were in an impossible situation. What were you supposed to do?"

Angry tears welled up in her eyes and her teeth clenched with her anger and shame. But she brushed the tears away with a swipe of her hand, squared her shoulders and faced Devlin, ready for whatever happened next.

"Stop!" she yelled. "Stop being so understanding! You don't know! It's so much worse than you think," she managed to say, her voice now barely above a whisper.

"Tell me," he urged, his voice low and steady. "Whatever it is, Rosalind, tell me."

Rosalind took a deep breath, the memory of that night crashing over her like a wave. "I didn't just lie to you," she confessed, her voice breaking. "I killed him. I murdered Edmond."

Devlin's expression still didn't change—he remained still. He said nothing, only waited.

Rosalind's whole body started to shake; her words tumbled out in a flood of emotion. "That night...the night he disappeared, Edmond had beaten me. Severely. I knew I couldn't stay any longer. I ran. I took my horse, and I rode, not knowing where I was going—just away from him."

She paused, her breath ragged, the memory of Edmond's violence still fresh in her mind. Devlin stood motionless, listening.

"Edmond followed me. He wasn't far behind. But he didn't know the land as well as I did. He took the wrong path, the one that leads into the mire. His horse got stuck. Edmond had either fallen off or dismounted, sinking up to his belly in the muck. I rode on, leaving him there. I didn't care what happened to him at that moment. I was just so desperate to get away." Rosalind's voice faltered and she swallowed hard, the weight of her next words almost too much to bear.

"But I turned back. I don't know why. Perhaps a part of me wanted to help him. When I returned, I found my uncle struggling to free himself. He was sinking. His horse was gone, and he was alone... terrified." Her voice wavered, tears streaming down her cheeks as she forced herself to continue. "I tried to help him. I didn't have a rope, so I reached for him, but he cursed me, Devlin. He cursed me like he'd never before. He said I'd regret running from him. He grabbed me and snagged my locket, trying to pull me down with him."

Devlin's gaze darkened, and his grip on the locket tightened, but still, he said nothing.

Rosalind's voice dropped to a whisper; the words almost too painful to speak. "And so, I stopped trying. I backed away. I watched him sink further into the mire. I let him drown. I could've saved him, but I didn't. I left him there to die. He screamed after me, Devlin, over and over, but I never looked back. I rode back to the manor. I acted as though nothing had happened."

Silence filled the room, heavy and suffocating. Rosalind's heart pounded in her chest, and her pulse beat in her ears. She waited for Devlin to say something—anything.

"You... let him die."

Rosalind nodded, tears streaming freely down her face now. "Yes."

For a moment, Devlin remained still, his gaze locked on hers as though weighing the gravity of her confession. The silence stretched between them, unbearable, until finally, Devlin took a step toward her.

"You didn't murder him, Rosalind. You survived him. He was a monster, and you did the only thing you could to save yourself and protect the children. You said he beat you badly before you ran. Had he got free, he may have killed you the next time."

Rosalind blinked in disbelief. "But I let him die, Devlin. I could've saved him, and I didn't."

Devlin gently took her hand, his touch warm and grounding. "Rosalind, I would have done the same. No,

I would have done worse. I would have sat at the water's edge, toasted his upcoming demise with a mug of ale, and wished him a merry journey into Hell. Anyone who knew the truth of what he did to you would understand. You did what you had to do, and I don't blame you. Nothing you've told me changes how I feel about you."

She stared at him, her heart filled with a mixture of relief and disbelief. "You don't hate me?"

"I could never hate you," Devlin whispered, pulling her into his arms. "I love you. Nothing will ever change that."

Rosalind wept into his chest; the years of living in fear and the guilt and shame of that horrible night finally lifted. In Devlin's embrace, she was truly safe, and nothing would ever take that from her.

The tears flowed loudly and freely for some time, but once her sobs quieted, she lifted her head from his now wet shirt. She thought she saw several tear-glistened black lashes.

"You will never repeat what you just told me, Rosalind. I believe in my heart that you did what you had to do, but we are not sure everyone would feel the same. Does anyone else know?"

Rosalind shook her head, "No one but me, and now you."

"Good. We will keep it that way."

Then Devlin gifted her with a rare smile. "Now, let's go downstairs. We have a wedding to plan."

Rosalind smiled widely, and he continued with a mischievous grin.

"And there will be no long engagement as I won't be waiting long to be with you, Rosalind." He leaned down, and his mouth crushed hers in a long, warm kiss.

Rosalind couldn't agree more.

****

Benton watched his happy family. Rosalind had returned to the great hall with her husband-to-be. Soon she and Marta were planning a wedding and a return to Rosalind's estate. The children looked happier than he'd ever seen them and everyone talked, laughed, and played until the late hours of the night.

Once the household had retired to their chambers and the manor fell silent, Benton poured himself a goblet of wine and settled before the roaring fire. As the wine and the warmth of the fire soothed his aching body, his mind returned to the night of Edmond's disappearance.

His aging body had moved faster than usual, and his joints screamed with every step he made toward the stables. He knew he had to hurry. Tonight was different. Edmond was angrier than he'd ever seen him, and Rosalind once again bore the brunt of his dangerous mood.

Rosalind rode out like the devil chased her and Edmond followed. He trailed behind them, unseen, unheard, his old heart heavy with worry. Rosalind headed toward the bog. She knew the route well but it was dangerous at night.

At last, he reached the edge of the marsh and spotted Edmond. The lord was half-submerged in the mire, hurling curses and shouting for help. His eyes widened in surprise when Rosalind returned. She first hesitated at the edge of the muck, but then she waded in and reached out, yelling at him to grab her hand. Edmond's words were vile, hateful, filled with threats.

The old man's jaw clenched. Edmond had never deserved her.

Then he saw it—the moment Rosalind made her decision. The compassion for her drowning uncle was snuffed out like a candle in a brisk wind, and now she possessed a look of pity and sad resignation. She stepped back, and watched as Edmond struggled, sinking deeper into the thick, unforgiving mud.

He understood what this meant. Rosalind turned, struggling to get out of the mire, and once clear she rode back into the night as Edmond disappeared beneath the surface, his curses finally silenced forever.

He waited until she was gone before stepping forward. It was his duty to protect the Capell family. His breath was heavy, his limbs aching, but his mind was clear. He knew what had to be done. Rosalind had done what any woman in her place would have—she had survived. But now, there was a body to deal with, and if it was found, there would be questions.

Too many questions.

Slowly, he waded into the bog, grimacing as the mud sucked at his boots. All that could be seen of Edmond was one forearm floating above the black water. It took all his strength to pull the dead weight free from the shallow sink where it had lodged. He winced at Edmond's face, twisted in a grotesque snarl even in death.

He sighed as he looked down at Edmond. The night was thick around him, the air damp and cold, but he moved with purpose. He worked in silence, his old bones protesting with every movement, but his resolve never wavered. He gathered heavy stones that would sink the man in the deeper end of the bog.

Satisfied he'd added enough rocks to do the job, he pushed the body farther out into the water. He watched as Edmond disappeared.

The sky was beginning to lighten with the first hints of dawn by the time Benton mounted his horse again. He rode back to the manor in silence. What he had done would remain a secret. What he had done, he had done for the family—for Rosalind and for the Capell family name.

As the manor came into view, he straightened his back and rode through the gates. No one would ever know what had happened that night. Rosalind would be safe. The family would endure, as it always had.

He dismounted slowly, his body aching with every step, and returned to his quarters. He washed the mud from his hands and changed his clothes. His heart was heavy, but he had no regrets.

This was his duty, after all.

A word about the author...

Beth Price is a former elementary school teacher turned writer living in the foothills of Appalachia. When not crafting stories or diving into books across all genres, Beth enjoys tending her thriving garden, hiking, and crocheting. She and her husband love traveling the country in their camper van, embracing adventure and gathering inspiration for future tales and novels from the places they visit.

****

If you enjoyed this story, leaving a review at your favorite book retailer or reader website would be much appreciated. Thank you!